"Hey, it's all right. You're okay. Everything's going to be okay."

Patrick was beside her now, his voice confident and reassuring as he leaned over her and gathered her into his arms. Charli didn't think she'd ever felt anything as wonderful as his embrace. After more than forty hours trapped and alone, to have someone close enough to touch, close enough to feel the warmth of his breath on her cheek, was overwhelming. "We'll do this together, okay?"

She nodded. "Okay."

"We're going to take it slow."

"I just want to get out of here."

"I know you do, and don't worry, that's the next thing on my list, but we don't want to move you too quickly. Trust me."

He was still holding her hand, and his dark green eyes didn't leave her face as he waited for her to agree.

She nodded.

Dear Reader,

I can't believe this is my thirtieth medical romance! I love the fact that my dreams and daydreams are still being published, and I thank you so much for choosing to read my books.

This is a story that has been in my head for a while now and it's a bit of a departure from the usual category romances, but I thought, after so many stories, maybe it was the right time to write this one.

Like so many of my books, the inspiration for my characters came from a real-life story that became a "what if this happened next" idea in my head.

If you remember the 1997 Thredbo landslide disaster in New South Wales, Australia, my hero and heroine have grown from the stories of the many people involved in the rescue efforts. Special ops paramedic Patrick Reeves is the perfect hero: tall, dark and handsome, he rescues people for a living, but it hasn't stopped him from being touched by tragedy.

I needed to find him a heroine, but he ended up finding her himself.

Thanks to my editors, who let me take this one a little left of center!

If you enjoy this story or have enjoyed any of my others, I'd love to hear from you. You can visit my website, emily-forbesauthor.com, or drop me a line at emilyforbes@internode.on.net.

Emily

RESCUED BY THE SINGLE DAD

EMILY FORBES

HARLEQUIN® MEDICAL ROMANCE™

Recycling programs
for this product may
not exist in your area.

ISBN-13: 978-1-335-64143-4

Rescued by the Single Dad

First North American Publication 2019

Copyright © 2019 by Emily Forbes

Printed in U.S.A.

Books by Emily Forbes

Harlequin Medical Romance

The Christmas Swap

Waking Up to Dr. Gorgeous

The Hollywood Hills Clinic

Falling for the Single Dad

Tempted & Tamed

A Doctor by Day…
Tamed by the Renegade
A Mother to Make a Family

A Kiss to Melt Her Heart
His Little Christmas Miracle
A Love Against All Odds
One Night That Changed Her Life
Falling for His Best Friend

Visit the Author Profile page
at Harlequin.com for more titles.

For Beck

Thank you for many years of fun, laughter and fabulous friendship. Wishing you a very happy and very big birthday! I look forward to celebrating this one and many others with you.

Love,
Emily

10 March 2019

**Praise for
Emily Forbes**

"*A Mother to Make a Family* is a lovely story about second chances with life and love…. A well written, solid tale of sweet love and charming family."

—*Goodreads*

CHAPTER ONE

CHARLI SLID OUT from the booth as a waitress delivered pizzas to the table. She had only been in Australia for two days and was still suffering the effects of jet-lag after the long flight east. Her body clock was telling her she'd been up all night and her stomach heaved at the thought of pizza for breakfast, even though it was just a little after ten p.m.

Her sister and her friends looked as though they were preparing to kick on and Charli needed something soft to drink if she was going to last any longer. Amy and her fellow ski instructors seemed to be able to hold their drinks far better than Charli ever could. She'd heard the Australians partied hard and she doubted she'd keep up even if she wasn't exhausted.

She couldn't remember the last time she'd had a decent night's sleep. It felt like years ago. She'd spent the past seven years studying hard and working part time in her hours off. While she'd had plenty of late nights, very few had been because she'd been out having fun. Medical school had been hugely demanding of both her time and effort, and her two years of Foundation Training had been even more exhausting. Sleep had been hard to come by for many years and, most recently, it had been thanks to her lousy ex, but she'd come to Australia to forget about him and she refused to waste any more time thinking about past mistakes. She'd make a trip to the bar and order a round of drinks and then maybe no one would notice if she sneaked away early.

The bar was crowded, the crush of the *après-ski* crowd several people deep, and Charli could feel herself swaying on her feet as she waited to be served. Her eyes drifted closed, just briefly, but it was long enough to cause her to lose her balance and stumble. She staggered backwards, bumping into the person behind her. Large hands grabbed at her elbows, steadying her.

'Whoa, are you okay?'

She heard a deep voice in her ear. She

turned around and looked up into a pair of very dark eyes.

She blinked as she tried to clear her head. She felt foggy, disoriented and she focussed hard. Her first thought was that this man who had her by the elbows was cute. About her age, several inches taller than her, maybe a smidge over six feet, with messy dark hair to go with his dark eyes.

'Are you okay?'

She could see his lips moving, she could see his teeth, which were even and white in contrast to the shadow of a beard on his jaw. She heard him speak but the combination of jet-lag and his broad Australian accent meant it took her a few moments to translate his words into something she could make sense of. She nodded. 'Yes, sorry about that.'

'Are you sure you should be ordering more drinks?'

'They're for my friends.'

He raised one dark eyebrow and she noticed he had a small scar just under his left eye. She must be standing way too close if she could notice that but the crowd around her, coupled with the fact that he was still holding onto her, meant she couldn't move away. His hands were warm and gentle and she found she didn't actually want to step away.

'I promise,' she said. 'I'm having a lemonade. I'm just jet-lagged.'

'In that case, let me order for you. What else can I get you?'

'A jug of beer—'

'And a lemonade,' he added as he dropped his hands and turned towards the bar.

Charli nodded as she pulled her purse from her handbag, wishing he hadn't let go of her. She still felt a little unsteady but this time she didn't think it was solely because of the jet-lag. She studied his back as he placed the order. Her eyes took in the breadth of his shoulders and the way his hair curled over the collar of his T-shirt. His shirt fit him snugly, showing off his muscular physique. She lifted her eyes up to his as he turned back from the bar. 'How much will it be?' she asked.

'Twenty bucks should cover it.'

'Twenty? What colour is that again?'

'Orange.'

'I'm still getting used to your money,' she said as she fished in her purse for the colourful note. 'It's pretty.'

'You're English?'

She nodded. 'Just arrived. Hence the jet-lag,' she said, holding out the note. He reached for the money with his left hand and her fingers tingled as she placed the note in his hand. She noticed he wasn't wearing a wedding ring. Maybe her jet-lag wasn't as bad as she'd thought.

'Whereabouts are you from?' he asked her.

'London. Have you been there?'

'I have.'

'Did you like it?'

'To be completely honest, I prefer it here. Fewer people, better weather.' He smiled at her, softening his words, but she wasn't offended. He'd probably be able to say anything that he liked without upsetting people as long as he said it with a smile. His smile was wide, making his eyes crinkle at the corners and his mouth turn up at the edges. It suited him.

'In case you haven't noticed,' she said, 'you're in the snow. Snow is snow all around the world.' Somehow, she managed to continue the conversation even though she was distracted.

'Yes, but in Australia we choose to go to the snow, we don't have to put up with it unless we want to, and even in the snow we get our fair share of sunny days. There's nothing better than wearing a T-shirt and getting a sun tan while you ski.'

'You ski in a T-shirt?'

Her eyes roamed over him again, taking in the view from the front this time. It was even better than the back. His chest was broad, his stomach flat, his arms were tanned and muscular, lightly covered with dark hair—enough to be masculine, not enough to be off-putting—and his skin was olive. His T-shirt hugged his chest and abdominals and was tucked into a pair of red ski pants that had some official-looking emblem on them, but she couldn't make out what it said in the dim lighting of the bar.

'You bet.' He spoke in the same laid-back, friendly manner that Amy's friends used. Unhurried, relaxed. She'd have to get used to the Aussie way of speaking.

He paid for their order but made no move to pick up his drinks and leave the bar.

'Hey, Reeves, a man is not a camel!'

Charli saw him turn his head at the comment. She followed the direction of his gaze and saw a group of men, all wearing the same navy and red uniform, standing around a tall round table. 'Are they talking to you?' she asked.

'Afraid so.'

'I'd better let you go,' she said, hoping he'd say he'd stay. 'Thank you for your help.'

'It was my pleasure...' He paused and she knew he was waiting for her name.

'Charli.'

'Charli,' he repeated. She liked the way it sounded when he said it. 'Maybe I'll see you around.'

She hoped so, she thought as she took the jug of beer and her lemonade back to the booth, sliding in next to her sister.

'Who was that?' Amy asked.

'I don't know,' she said, realising belatedly that she had no idea. She had a name but no idea if it was his first or last.

'I bet he could take your mind off your troubles for the next few days,' her sister added.

Charli smiled but shook her head. She'd decided she was a terrible judge of character but even she could tell he had trouble written all over him. He was cute and confident and his smile had made her knees wobble, but she suspected he had that effect on a lot of women and she wasn't about to let him add her to his list. 'I'm not looking for someone from ski patrol to take my mind off things.'

'You should be, he was hot. But he's not ski patrol, their uniform is red and white, not red and navy.'

'Do you know what he does?' She should have got more information, she thought, even as she tried to tell herself she wasn't interested. The last thing she needed was a rebound fling with a hot stranger. But she couldn't deny he'd caught her attention.

Amy shook her head before she was dragged back into conversation with one of the other ski instructors, a handsome, blond Canadian. It looked as though Amy might get her own distraction tonight.

Charli scanned the room but she couldn't see the cute guy or his friends from where she sat, and she wasn't about to go looking for him. She needed to clear her head, not complicate it, but if she *had* been looking she suspected he was just the type she would have fallen for. It would be safer if she just took herself back to Amy's apartment and got a decent night's sleep. Tomorrow was another day.

She leant over to Amy. 'I think I might

call it a night,' she said as she picked up her jacket.

'Really?'

'I'm tired.'

'I'll come with you,' Amy said as she started to stand.

'No, no, don't leave on my account.'

But Amy was already up and had tucked her arm through Charli's elbow. 'You've come all this way to see me, Canadian Dan will understand.' She smiled and raised an eyebrow. 'Unless you're going to find that hot guy and don't want me cramping your style?'

Charli shook her head. 'No, I'm going home to bed, alone. I'm tired of being disappointed by men, I'd rather just go to bed with my fantasies than find out that the reality isn't what I hoped for.'

'Oh, Charli.' Amy sighed as she hugged her younger sister close. 'I know Hugo hurt you but not all men are bastards.'

'Maybe not, but I'm not game to find out tonight.'

'Well, let me know if you change your mind. There are plenty of cute guys here who will happily let you try out your fantasies on them.'

Charli laughed. 'Seriously, I'm fine. I'll go and tuck myself into bed and I'll see you in the morning.' She kissed her sister's cheek and gently pushed her back into her seat. 'There's no need for both of us to have an early night. Stay, have fun.'

She'd meant it when she'd said she wasn't looking for a man to take her mind off things but, even so, she couldn't resist one last glance around the bar on her way out.

He was still there.

He was leaning against the wall, surrounded by his mates, but he was watching her. Her heart skittered as his eyes locked onto hers. He straightened up and her step faltered as he put his glass on the table and moved towards her. Somehow she managed to keep walking but her eyes didn't leave his. He weaved through the crowd, his path at an angle to hers, and she knew he would reach her before she got to the door.

He waited for her and she stopped beside him, her feet deciding her course of action for her.

'Are you leaving?' His voice was calm and his dark eyes held her gaze, making her feel as though he could see into the depths of her soul.

She nodded.

'Will you stay and have a drink with me?'

Should she? She wanted to but she really didn't trust herself to make good decisions. Even when she wasn't jet-lagged, she made terrible ones. 'I don't even know your name.' She stalled for time.

'It's Patrick. Patrick Reeves.'

He continued to watch her closely and the rest of the crowd faded into insignificance as she hugged the sound of his name to herself. It was a nice name and he had an even nicer face and a fabulous smile. She was tempted, very tempted, but she was also exhausted. 'I don't think I'll be very good company,' she said, barely able to string two words together, although whether that was the effect of jet-lag or Patrick's intense gaze she wasn't sure.

'May I walk you home, then?'

She hesitated, but only briefly. She knew she'd regret it if she walked out alone. She nodded. Decision made. 'I'd like that.'

He held her jacket for her, helping her into it. 'Where are you staying?' he asked as they left the bar and he shrugged into his insulated jacket.

'At Snowgum Chalet, with my sister.' Her boots slipped on the icy path and Patrick reached out to steady her, wrapping an arm around her waist, catching her before she could fall. He lifted her slightly, settling her back on her feet.

'Thank you.' He still had his arm around her and her tongue felt too big in her mouth, making her stumble over the words. 'I seem to have trouble keeping my feet around you.'

He knew the feeling. She was looking up at him with big blue eyes. His heart missed a beat and he felt like he was falling too. 'I'll have to remember to watch out for you on the slopes,' he said as he took her hand. It was small but fitted perfectly into his grip and he tucked it into his elbow. 'I have a feeling you could be dangerous.'

'I'm usually okay on skis,' she replied, completely missing his meaning, 'but I am very wobbly today. I'm sure I'll be all right after a decent sleep. Are you skiing tomorrow?'

He shook his head. 'Unfortunately not.'

'Do you work here? I saw your friends were all wearing the same uniform.'

'Not exactly,' he said as he changed direction, taking a path to the right that turned past Ironbark Lodge and headed down the hill to Snowgum Chalet. 'We're all paramedics, we've been doing alpine training exercises here. We're part of the High Country Special Operations arm.'

'That sounds exciting. What did you have to do?'

'Avalanche training, helicopter drops into the back country, abseiling down cliffs, that sort of thing.'

'Exciting *and* exhausting.'

He supposed it was both but there was nothing unusual in the hectic pace of his life. Working as a Special Ops paramedic meant his life moved rapidly from one disaster to another and he embraced the pace, especially over the past two years. Being busy meant he didn't have time to think. Didn't have time to dwell on things.

'It's been challenging,' he admitted as they reached the front door of her lodge, 'but it's exhilarating too.'

It had been busy and he was knackered.

He should be going home to bed, not chatting up pretty strangers in the snow, but he'd been powerless to resist her. He could count on one hand the number of women he'd bothered to look at twice since losing his wife two years ago. There had been no shortage of offers, plenty of women seemed to find the idea of a widower romantically attractive, but he had barely given any of them the time of day. Initially he'd been too grief-stricken, then he'd felt as if he was being unfaithful, and lately he'd been too busy. But something about Charli had struck a chord with him; something about her had made him sit up and take notice.

He was getting lonely. Shift work and a three-year-old daughter occupied a lot of his time but there were nights when he was home, alone on the couch while his daughter slept, and he missed adult company. Female company. He wanted a connection, it didn't need to be permanent, but finding someone attractive was an unusual experience for him and that flutter of anticipation, that curiosity, that tremor of excitement, had been enough to galvanise him into action. When he'd seen her heading for the door he'd known he couldn't let her leave without talking to her once more. He knew that if he let her walk out of the bar he would never see her again.

Charli let go of his hand as she searched in her bag for the key. She turned to him and for the briefest of moments he thought about what he'd say if she invited him in.

He was leaving tomorrow. At best, they could have one night together. But he didn't get the impression that outcome was on the cards and he didn't know if he would accept the invitation if it was forthcoming.

'Do you think we could have that drink tomorrow night?' she asked.

He should have been relieved that her words weren't the ones he'd half hoped to hear. A lack of an invitation meant he didn't have to wrestle with his conscience, didn't have to remind himself of all the reasons why he should say goodnight and go home to his own bed. She'd made the decision for him. He should be grateful but he couldn't help feeling disappointed.

'I'd love to but I have to go back to Melbourne.' He was due to leave first thing in the morning but the disappointment left a sour taste in his mouth. Maybe he could postpone his departure for just a few hours? He'd have to make some phone calls, ask for more favours, but it would be worth it. He had to try. 'Could I take you to brunch instead, or are you planning to be out skiing bright and early?'

'No, brunch sounds lovely.' She smiled up at him and made him wonder if it was too soon to kiss her goodnight.

He'd known her less than an hour. He figured it probably was too soon.

'Great,' he said as he resisted temptation and waited for her to unlock her door to her ground-floor apartment. He had no reason to delay the farewell any longer. 'I'll meet you here at ten.'

He headed towards his bed, feeling unexpectedly hopeful and positive.

Snow blanketed the ground beneath his boots but the evening sky was clear and dark. There were no clouds and no moon but hundreds of tiny stars studded the darkness, relieving the blackness. He stopped outside the bar and the background hum of the alpine resort village faded as he closed his eyes and breathed deeply, inhaling the fresh mountain air. The scent of snow gums, wood smoke and barbeque filled his nose.

He stood still for a moment longer, soaking up the atmosphere.

The lights reflected off the snow as the machine operators traversed the slopes, smoothing out the ski runs ready for tomorrow, but he turned his back on the runs and looked instead past the chalets and buildings of the Wombat Gully Ski Resort and further up the mountain where the stately snow gums lined the ski runs. They stood sentinel, their trunks smooth and ghostly white, lit only by the light coming from the lodges. There was no wind to rustle their leaves, the air was still and so was he.

He knew he was okay. He'd kept things together for two years and had come through the worst of it. He was managing as a single parent. It wasn't easy, far from it, but it was getting better. He had a routine, he had good support and he and his daughter had formed their own duo. Three had become two but two was okay. They were doing all right. Two was better than one. And he had a career he loved. He knew it could be all-consuming but it had saved him from depression and misery and had given him something else to focus on. Between his work and Ella, he had everything he needed. Not everything he *wanted* but life was good. He was doing okay.

Opening his eyes, he took in the natural beauty that surrounded him and thought, for the first time in years, that it was good to be alive. No, not thought but believed. There was a difference.

He breathed out and his warm breath condensed into white puffs of steam in the frigid air. He'd put his life on hold since Margie's unexpected death, concentrating on his daughter and on his career, and his personal life had been largely ignored. Perhaps it was time to look to the future.

Patrick ignored the drone of the snow groomers and the constant thrumming of the snow-making machines and the music drifting into the night from the bar behind him—none of that was anything to do with him—as his thoughts drifted back to Charli. He would meet her for brunch. It felt odd to be organising a date but also exciting. After that he would return to Melbourne but at least he would have taken a step forward. A step towards a future. He and Ella couldn't remain a pair for ever, he didn't believe that was healthy. To move forward he had to get back into the dating game. But he wanted to do it on his terms. He wanted to wait until he felt a connection with someone. Charli was a promising start.

'Hey, Pat, you calling it a night?'

Pat turned, his self-reflection interrupted by Connor Green, one of his colleagues, who was headed his way.

'Yep.' He waited to see if Connor had been sent to try to persuade him to return to the bar. He was out of luck if that was his mission. The team was close-knit and Pat had become good friends with his teammates over the years. They'd provided great support to him, but he wanted a clear head for tomorrow.

'Me too,' Connor replied.

A sudden gust of wind swirled around Pat as Connor spoke, startling him after the extraordinary stillness of the night. A noise similar to that of a jet engine roared behind them, its sound swallowing the background noise, and the ground shook beneath their feet. Pat looked up but the sky was just as dark as before. He could see nothing untoward but the rumble continued, the ground unsteady, testing their balance. He felt his heart rate accelerate as he turned around, his eyes glued to the mountain, searching for the source of the noise, his gut telling him it wasn't a plane.

Was it an avalanche? Even though they'd spent hours on avalanche training he'd never heard, or seen, one. They were a rare occurrence in Australia.

His eyes scanned the slopes, glancing over the buildings as he looked towards the tree line. Ironbark Lodge sat highest on the mountain and he could see it silhouetted against the snow, its windows lit up against the night sky. He saw the lights waver and flicker as though candles illuminated the glass instead of electricity. And then the lights disappeared, leaving the lodge in darkness.

Pat looked down the mountain, expecting a complete power outage, but the other buildings remained bright. Movement in the corner of his eye drew his gaze up again.

He blinked.

Ironbark Lodge looked as if it was moving.

He must be more tired than he thought. He shook his head and rubbed one hand across his eyes before opening them again. He must be seeing things.

No. He wasn't. The lodge was definitely moving.

'Bloody hell!' It took him a moment to process what he was looking at and meanwhile Ironbark Lodge continued to move. He watched on in horror and disbelief as the lodge slid down the side of the mountain.

Snowgum Chalet sat directly in its path.

He took off, sprinting along the icy paths, retracing his steps from moments before, running right into the path of the disaster.

CHAPTER TWO

'AMY?' CHARLI CALLED from the darkness of
the bedroom.

She'd fallen asleep quickly with a smile on
her lips as she'd thought about having brunch
with Patrick but had been woken abruptly
by the wind. 'Amy, are you there? Can you
hear that?'

The wind was loud. So loud it sounded like
it was rushing through the apartment. At first,
she'd thought the noise was the bathroom fan
but as it continued to increase in volume she
realised it wasn't coming from the bathroom
but was moving closer. It sounded like it was
coming for her. She sat up just as a loud explosion split the air and her heart leapt as the
unexpected sound shattered the night.

What was that? A gas cylinder exploding?
A car backfiring?

The windows of the apartment rattled as

she reached for the bedside lamp. The whole bed was shaking and it took her two attempts to find the switch. A backfiring car wouldn't shake the bed.

But an avalanche might.

'Amy?' she called again, louder this time, as she finally turned on the light.

Was Amy home or was she still in the bar? Charli was about to get out of bed to look for her when the lights went out, engulfing her in darkness.

The noise hadn't stopped, it had only intensified.

It was incredible. It sounded like a freight train, which was impossible as there was no train on the mountain. Her next thought was perhaps it was one of the snow-grooming machines. Had someone lost control? And then, cutting through the noise, she heard screams.

'Amy?'

She leapt out of bed, stumbling in the darkness.

The noise was deafening now. Windows shattered and she heard glass hit the floor. Timbers were cracking and metal twisted and screeched, hurting her ears. She could hear bricks falling and over it all the noise of the wind and the screams continued.

Instinctively she threw her hands over her head as she took another step forward before her legs gave way beneath her. She didn't realise that it wasn't her legs but the floor that had disappeared from under her, and then there was nothing.

No light. No sound and only very slight vibrations. The wind had stopped as suddenly as it had begun and the room was no longer shaking violently, but she still couldn't see and, much worse, she still couldn't hear a sound. Even the screams had been silenced.

'Amy?'

She coughed as she inhaled a mouthful of dust and it stuck on her tongue.

'Are you there?'

There was only silence. Had Amy come home? Was she there?

Charli had no idea. It was awfully quiet.

Deathly quiet.

The room had stopped shaking and was now resting quietly in the dark. But the sudden silence wasn't peaceful or calming, it was frightening. What had happened?

The air was frigid. The temperature had

dropped and the floor beneath her legs was cold and damp. The bedroom was carpeted but the carpet was now flooded and icy water swirled around her. She could feel it and it chilled her to the bone, but she had no idea where it had come from.

'Hello. Is anyone there?' she yelled, choking on the thick dust that seemed to be hanging in the air.

She tried to stand up but smacked her head on something hard before she could fully straighten her knees. She swore out loud and rubbed her forehead above her left eye. A lump was already forming from the collision. She crouched down and reached up with one hand. She felt concrete under her fingers. Was that the ceiling? Why was it so low?

She squatted on the floor as she tried to figure out what had happened. Had the ceiling collapsed? God, she hoped not. Amy's apartment was on the ground floor of a four-storey building.

What had happened? It was impossible to tell. The darkness made it impossible to get her bearings, impossible to work out what had happened and what was going on.

She reached out carefully, not knowing what she might find.

There was nothing in front of her so she crawled towards the door, or to where she thought the door was. Her hands were immersed in the freezing cold water and her fingers were going numb. She was dressed only in a T-shirt and knickers, clothes that were warm enough to sleep in while the central heating worked, but it offered no protection in her current situation.

She stretched her hands out and shuffled forward on her knees. There was an overpowering smell of diesel fumes and overflowing toilets. She didn't want to know what she was crawling through.

Something sharp grazed her calf but she pressed on, hands outstretched in front of her.

It felt like she'd gone no further than a few feet before she ran into a wall. She was sure the door had to be there somewhere. She moved sideways, still calling Amy's name, as she felt for a gap, her fingers searching for the door frame. She cried out as something pierced her palm, slicing into the flesh beneath her right thumb. The wound throbbed and she could feel blood running down to her elbow. She ignored the warm blood as she felt more frantically for the doorway but there was no gap. Instead she found herself wedged into a corner.

She was confused, disoriented but she continued to inch her way around the room.

She kept her hands outstretched, fearful of hitting her head again in the darkness. She breathed in the putrid, frigid air as she crawled through the darkness.

Her hands met more cold concrete. It was rough under her fingers, the smooth walls obliterated, leaving what felt like a pile of rubble. The ceiling pressed down on her head, making her feel claustrophobic. She fought back a wave of panic. Where was she? Nothing was familiar.

'Amy? Are you here?' She was sobbing now, crying salty tears that ran down her cheeks and mingled with the dust that caked her mouth.

She forced herself to keep moving. She couldn't stay still. She had to find a way out of there before she froze to death.

She moved a few more feet and her fingers made contact with smooth metal. Was that the bed frame? Had she done a full circle? The bed had a high metal bed head. She traced the frame. The poles were bent, the frame leaning in towards the centre of the bed. She reached up and felt the ceiling. Somehow the metal bed head was supporting the ceiling. A concrete ceiling that should be five feet above her head, not several inches.

How had the bed not collapsed completely?

She was lucky she hadn't been crushed, she thought, before she had a more terrifying realisation. But what about Amy? Where *was* her sister? What might have happened to her?

'Amy?' she whispered. Scared now of what she might *not* hear. Listening in hope for her sister's voice.

Still nothing.

The carpet was sodden and sludgy under her knees. Crawling through freezing mud and water in the dark wasn't getting her anywhere. She needed to see. She needed light. She felt for the bedside table, reaching for her mobile phone that had been resting on top. She desperately needed the flashlight function, but her hand met empty air. There was no table and she could only assume her phone now lay submerged in the vile water that lapped at her thighs.

She moved around the other side of the bed, only to find herself in another dead end. There was no way around this. She was trapped in a windowless, flooded tomb.

How had she ended up here?

What had happened?

Had a snow groomer crashed into their apartment? What had happened to the apartments above?

She had no idea.

All she knew was that she was trapped, buried alive.

She wanted to scream but the air was still so cold and so thick with dust she didn't want to breathe it in.

Stay calm. Think.

She wanted to be warm.

Crawling back to the bed, she curled into a ball and tucked her injured hand under her armpit in an attempt to stop the bleeding and to warm herself up. She tugged the quilt over her, it was cold but dry and although she still wasn't warm at least she wasn't sitting in that filthy water.

She closed her eyes as she tried to figure out what to do. She wanted to get out of there but had no idea how she would achieve that.

Amy would know.

She let her tears flow as she lay in the darkness.

She wanted her sister.

Pat only had one thought as he ran towards Snowgum Chalet.

Charli.

He had to warn her. Had to get her out.

He skidded to a stop and gulped a lungful of frigid air as he tried to comprehend what he was seeing.

Ironbark Lodge was sliding almost gracefully down the slope, seemingly with no great urgency, keeping pace with the eucalyptus trees that were falling alongside it. It left a dark smear of mud in its wake as it pushed the snow ahead like a gigantic snowplough. The bottom floors of the building were pushed out as it gathered momentum and the upper levels toppled backwards. The accompanying sound was an agonising, horrific cracking of timbers, an explosion of glass, a high-pitched shrieking of twisting metal and devastating human cries, but still the lodge continued to slide down the slope in front of him, heading straight for Snowgum Chalet. And Charli.

There was nothing he could do and he watched helplessly as the disaster unfolded before him until, with a sickening crash, the two lodges collided. Pat took a step forward, hopelessly, helplessly, as Snowgum Chalet collapsed like a deck of cards and the third and fourth stories crushed the floors below and sent a cloud of white concrete dust into the air.

Car alarms were blaring and, over the top of all the noise, the village distress siren wailed. The noise of the disaster brought people out of the buildings. They poured out of the surrounding bars, restaurants and lodges before stopping in their tracks, staring in disbelief at the site that confronted them. A dark muddy scar bisected the snow-covered mountain and an enormous pile of rubble, which moments before had been two buildings, dominated the landscape. They stared, momentarily frozen, at the ruins of the buildings that had, God only knew, how many people inside.

Pat could hear screams and calls for help coming from underneath the rubble. He had no idea how people had survived this disaster but clearly they had. He desperately hoped Charli had been one of them but he couldn't imagine how. Her apartment was— had been—on the ground floor. Unless she had somehow, miraculously, managed to escape, she was now buried under tonnes of concrete, bricks and steel. He fought back a wave of nausea as the dust cloud settled and he surveyed the scene. Everything had changed in an instant.

A few bystanders had already gathered their wits and were trying to move debris. There wasn't any discussion or any system to the recovery attempt, people simply started at the area closest to them. They stood in the mud, pulling at bricks and window frames, blocks of concrete and pieces of broken furniture. They looked like scavengers sorting through a rubbish tip. Nothing in front of them resembled a building.

He had to help. He pulled his gloves from the pocket of his jacket and shoved his hands into them as his feet began moving, propelling him towards the devastation. Muddy water continued to flow down the hill, making conditions underfoot slippery and treacherous. He could smell diesel fuel and sewage and gas but he couldn't stop. Charli's life might depend on him.

'Charli! Charli?'

For a split second he thought it was her voice he could hear. He turned around and saw a young woman flying down the path, her blonde hair streaming behind her.

Was it Charli?

She ran past Connor and Pat saw him grab at her. He held onto her, restraining her. Pat knew if he hadn't caught her she would have kept running.

She beat at his chest with her fists. 'Let me go. My sister is in there. I have to find her.'

His heart fell like a stone into his stomach, the last vestiges of hope shattered. It wasn't Charli. It was her sister.

He left Connor to deal with her as he stepped cautiously onto a teetering slab of concrete before thinking better of it when it wobbled under his feet. He didn't want to upset the balance. Who knew what lay beneath his feet.

He lay on his stomach and inched along the slab, listening to the cries for help and trying to work out where they were coming from. Sound bounced off the hard surfaces and off the mountain, distorting the voices and making it difficult to judge direction.

The darkness wasn't helping matters either. He couldn't see clearly, he couldn't tell if there were gaps in the rubble, any way in or out. He couldn't see survivors but he could hear them. He needed better light so he could tell where to start. He pulled his phone from his pocket, swiped the screen and pressed the flashlight icon but the light it gave off was pathetic.

'I need some light over here. Does anyone have a torch?' The lights of the village had been bright enough to see the buildings topple but they weren't bright enough now. He needed stronger beams, much stronger. The headlights from a car or a snowplough.

'Pat, what the hell are you doing? It's not safe, man.'

He heard Connor's voice from behind him. He turned his head. He could see dozens of people gathered in the semi-darkness, torches and phones causing multiple circles of light. 'Pass me a torch.'

'No. You need to come back. We need to assess the situation. It's too dangerous.'

'I can hear people. I need to see if I can reach them.'

'And what if that slab gives way under you? We could lose you along with anyone trapped under there,' Connor responded. 'We need a plan.'

Pat ignored him. He knew Connor wouldn't risk coming out after him. Two people on this teetering slab would be asking for trouble. Pat could stay out there safe in the knowledge that no one could drag him back. He knew he was taking a risk but what choice did he have? People were trapped. They needed his help.

'Hello? Can you hear me?' he called out.

'Yes.'

'I'm trapped.'

'Help us.' One, two, three different voices called back to him.

But none of them belonged to Charli.

He didn't want to stop but he couldn't ignore these cries for assistance. 'Are you hurt?'

'My wife. You have to help me. I can't reach her.'

'I'm stuck, my leg is caught. There's water coming in. I can't move. Help me, please, help me.'

There were only two replies to his question.

'Who is there? Can you tell me your names?'

'Simon.' The voice was faint and Pat strained to listen. Where were the other voices? Where was the husband? His wife?

'Pat, you need to follow protocol. It's not safe,' Connor called out, urging him to rethink his position.

Pat knew he was right. But knowing Connor was right wasn't enough to get him to pull back. He could argue that this wasn't a training drill or an official rescue. Not yet. He was effectively just a bystander, a good Samaritan, and his first instinct was to help. He would be careful. If he thought he was in danger, or there was a risk of causing further harm, he'd pull back.

'Think about Ella,' Connor called to him. 'What happens to her if something happens to you?'

Pat hesitated, knowing Connor had won this round. He was being foolish, he wasn't just risking his own safety, he was risking more than that, he was risking Ella's life as she knew it. Ella was all he had left and he had to stay safe for her.

Connor hadn't needed to come after him

at all. He had won the battle of wills with a few well-chosen words.

'Simon?' Pat called out. 'I'll be back, I need to get help.'

'Don't leave me here.'

Simon's voice called back to him, begging him not to go. One voice only. What had happened to the others? Had they lost consciousness? Or worse? Could they hear but not respond? Would Simon notice the silence?

Pat wanted to stay but he knew it was impossible to perform this rescue without equipment and help. 'I promise I'll be back.'

But he couldn't promise he'd be back in time.

He closed his eyes and pictured Ella's face and knew he had no option. It ripped him in two to leave but he had no choice.

He turned and began to inch his way off the slab. He had moved less than a foot when the ground wobbled and shifted and the concrete under him trembled and vibrated. His heart was in his throat as adrenalin surged through his body and he fought to keep his balance.

'Reeves,' Connor yelled at him. 'Get back here!'

CHAPTER THREE

CHARLI WOKE WITH a start. Something wet dripped from the ceiling, hitting her forehead.

She frowned, perplexed, and lifted her hand to wipe the moisture from her skin. She winced as her fingers brushed across her hairline. There was a large bump over her left eye and her skin felt tacky. And then she remembered where she was and what had happened.

She was freezing and her hand was throbbing. She'd torn a strip of fabric off the bedsheet and wrapped it around the base of her right thumb to stem the bleeding, but she hadn't been able to see how bad the wound was and her fingers were too cold to be able to give her any sensory feedback but she thought it had stopped bleeding.

The room was still pitch black, giving her no clue as to the time. She hadn't meant to fall asleep. She was thirsty and freezing and worried. She'd never treated anyone with hypothermia but she knew it was a real danger. She was curled in a ball on the bed, nestled into the small gap between the collapsed roof and the crushed bedhead. The quilt covered her but it was doing little to keep her warm.

Moisture continued to drip onto her head. She cupped her hands and let it gather in her palms. She lifted her hands to her face, wrinkling her nose in disappointment and disgust as she smelt the tainted water. It was undrinkable.

She tucked her hands under her armpits in a vain attempt to increase her body heat and lay in the dark, straining her ears to hear signs of life from anywhere around her. Was Amy in the apartment too? Had she fallen asleep and not heard Amy come home? Maybe her sister was there somewhere. Maybe she'd been knocked unconscious?

'Amy?' she whispered into the dark. In hope. Just in case, by some miracle, her sister was there.

Was that the sound of someone breathing?

Her heart rate spiked and she waited, listening carefully, before realising it was her own breathing she could hear, loud in the silence.

But then, in the distance, she heard another noise. A voice. People calling out, talking to each other. There *were* other people here, she wasn't alone!

'Hello? Can you hear me? *Hello?*'

There was no reply, the voices simply continued in the distance. They didn't stop or change or show any sign that they had heard her. No one replied to her and the words were indistinct. She knew they weren't close.

Her voice was hoarse, her throat parched and sore. No one was going to hear her. She needed to make more noise. But how?

She sat up slowly, uncurling herself like a fern frond, and hesitantly felt for the floor with her cold, bare feet. Her toes were tiny blocks of ice, she had some sensation in the two biggest toes but nothing in the rest. How many hours had she been trapped here?

She should have stayed in the bar with Patrick. She should have had another lemonade. She couldn't remember now why it had been so necessary, so important that she get to bed. Maybe just a few more minutes' conversation would have delayed things enough so that she wouldn't have been in the apartment. But it was too late for those regrets now, she was in the apartment and she was alone.

She couldn't lie on the bed and wait to be found. She needed to *make* it happen. She needed to *do* something. Anything.

The carpet was sodden but no longer under water. She crawled across the damp, muddy floor as she felt around cautiously in the dark, searching for something she could use to create noise. Her hand throbbed where she had cut her palm but she ignored that. There were more important things to worry about. Her eyes hadn't become accustomed to the blackness, which she knew meant there was no light coming in. Did that mean there was also no fresh air? Would she suffocate before she was found?

Her thoughts lent urgency to her search. There were people out there, out beyond this tomb she was imprisoned in, and she needed them to find her. She couldn't contemplate dying in here. Someone would find her. She had to believe that. She wasn't ready to die. Not yet. She needed to alert people to her existence.

Lost in her thoughts, it took her a moment

to realise her fingers had closed around a slender object. A pole of some sort. It was cold to the touch, metal, not wood. It felt like a ski pole but she knew there weren't any in the room. It could be a piece of the bed, the rail from the wardrobe, part of the bedside lamp. She didn't know what it was or how it came to be lying on the floor. It didn't matter. All that mattered was that it would make more noise than she was capable of by yelling.

She crawled back to the bed. She could still hear noises from above but the voices were being drowned out by mechanical sounds now. She could feel her anxiety increasing with every passing second. What were they doing with those machines? What if they were bulldozers? What if they pushed more debris down on top of her? Her breaths came in short, rapid bursts as panic set in. She had to make some noise. They *had* to find her. Her panic gave strength to her cold, lethargic muscles and she hit the pole against the metal frame with as much energy as she could muster.

Her arm tired easily but she forced herself to continue.

One minute, two, she wasn't sure.

Lactic acid burned in her muscles and she stopped briefly, giving her arms a chance to rest. Her ears were ringing but she listened for noises from above. Something, anything, to let her know she'd been heard.

'Hello? Can anyone hear me?' she called, but her voice sounded faint even to her ears.

She heard a whistle, one long blast, that echoed around the mountain.

When it ceased, so had all the noise. Everything was silent.

What did it mean? Was it a warning whistle? Was there danger? Why was it so quiet?

She waited, the pole heavy in her hand. Where was everyone? Where had they gone?

Her heart beat furiously in her chest. She breathed deeply, trying to quell the rising panic that threatened to overwhelm her, but all she got was a lungful of stale, putrid air. The smell was vile and made her feel nauseous.

She let the pole fall from her fingertips.

What was coming her way now? More water? More mud?

Death?

She didn't know how much more she could

take. Her reserves were running low. She was exhausted, thirsty, hungry, sore, filthy and alone. Maybe it was easier just to let go.

She put her head down and cried and the tears gathered in the corner of her mouth. Ignoring the knowledge that her skin was covered in dust and who knew what else, she licked the tears from her lips. They were the only moisture she could get.

What would she do when her tears dried up?

She lay on the damp mattress in the dark and imagined dying alone. Buried here on the wrong side of the world.

Pat was exhausted. Since the landslide he'd slept for a total of eight out of the past thirty hours. He'd taken his assigned breaks but no more and, like all the search and rescue personnel, he was surviving on coffee and adrenalin.

Sixteen people had been listed as missing. In the past thirty hours, nine bodies had been recovered but not one survivor had been among them.

And Charli was still missing.

He had to believe that was good news.

There was still hope. Though he knew that the more time that passed the lower her chances of survival were, he wasn't going to give up. He'd made a silent promise to Charli that he wouldn't stop until he found her. It wasn't in his nature to give in and he refused to, even though hope was fading rapidly. There were still seven people to be found and he wasn't stopping until they'd all been accounted for.

Close to two thousand people were involved in the search and recovery effort but he'd made certain that he was assigned to the search zone that included the remains of Snowgum Chalet. The noise level on the mountain was high. Concrete drills and bobcats were the background noise to the sound of thousands of voices. At regular intervals a signal whistle blew and everyone downed tools and the mountain fell silent as they all held their collective breath and listened for any sound of survivors.

But the site remained eerily quiet. There was nothing at all to hear.

Even a concrete X-ray machine and thermal imaging equipment had so far failed to detect any trace of survivors.

Perhaps today their luck would turn.

At times he felt as though they were taking one step forward and two back. Between the fatigue and the lack of progress it was getting increasingly difficult to keep morale high. It was falling with every hour that passed but Pat knew that all it would take to lift everyone's spirits would be to find just one survivor. Just one. But low temperatures and exposure to the elements, combined with potential injuries, meant they didn't have a lot of time. Hypothermia, blood loss, fractures, organ damage—all of these could be fatal.

He tried to focus on the positives. There had been no further landslides and the skies remained clear. They didn't need snowfall to hamper their efforts.

He knew the negatives still outweighed the positives but despite the negative outcome of their efforts so far he refused to give in. Someone *must* have survived.

He swallowed the last mouthful of his breakfast before strapping himself into a harness in preparation for his stint working on the precariously steep slope. The mountain was wet, slippery and treacherous. His movements were slow and deliberate. It was imperative that he didn't dislodge the earth or other debris beneath him as there was the risk of the rubble giving way and sending him, and others, plunging down the mountainside. The process was like a game of Jenga or pick-up sticks. Moving or even touching the wrong piece could cause other pieces to fall and the result could be disastrous.

He'd been working for several hours with just a short break when the Sunday morning chapel bells rang out over the mountain. They'd been advised that today's service would give the volunteers, search-and-rescue crew and people who hadn't been evacuated from the mountain an opportunity to say a prayer for the dead and the missing, and anyone who wished to could put down tools and attend.

The site gradually went quiet as equipment was abandoned, machines switched off and work ceased as people made their way to the chapel.

'Did you want to come to the service?' Connor asked from his position alongside Pat.

Pat shook his head. 'You know I don't believe in God.' He'd given up on his tenuous belief two years ago when his prayers had gone unanswered. 'I think my time is better spent here, searching, doing something more practical.' He had a feeling something was about to happen. Something told him it was important to stay on site.

'Fair enough. But you can't search alone,' Connor said as he carefully shifted another piece of concrete. 'I'll stay too.'

Pat suspected a number of people were going to the chapel because they thought paying their respects was the right thing to do. He could understand their reasons but, in his mind, their attendance implied that they didn't expect to find anyone alive. He wasn't prepared to give up hope. Not yet. It was still possible. Each passing minute made it less likely but that was why it was so important to keep going. Until every missing person was accounted for, he wasn't going to give up. He nodded briefly, acknowledging Connor's offer. He wasn't going to try to talk him out of it. Protocol dictated that they work in pairs. He needed Connor if he wanted to continue.

The bells stopped ringing as the search zone was vacated, leaving Pat and Connor alone in their small section. They worked in silence, their movements methodical as they continued to clear their small area. As Pat pulled at a piece of broken and twisted window frame he heard a metallic ping. He threw the debris over his shoulder, assuming his movements had made the noise, but as the metal flew through the air he heard a second ping.

He looked around the site. There were a few people still working but no one nearby. He knew that sound on the mountain carried long distances and echoed. The sound could have come from anywhere but in the silence that had descended on the site he felt his hopes lift.

'Did you hear that?' he asked Connor.

'Hear what?'

Pat was kneeling on the rubble but went completely still as he listened again.

'What was it?' Connor said.

Pat held up a hand. 'Hang on a minute.' But there was nothing more.

'Hello? Can you hear me?' He called out across the site. He could hear the expectation and excitement in his voice. He waited, still and silent, and his heart skipped a beat as he heard a reply.

'Can you hear...?'

'There! That.' He turned to look at Connor but his friend was shaking his head.

'It's just an echo.'

Was it his imagination playing tricks? He was tired, they all were, but he knew it was something important. 'I don't think so.' He called again. 'Hello?'

'Please. Help me.'

Pat turned back to Connor. 'Tell me you heard that?'

Connor's eyes were wide with surprise as he nodded.

Pat grinned. He could feel his smile splitting his face in two. 'We've got someone!'

CHAPTER FOUR

PAT INCHED CAREFULLY across the concrete slab that might have once been a ceiling or a floor or even a wall. He reined in his eagerness, making sure his movements were slow and deliberate. The engineers had deemed the site safe but still he was cautious.

'Hello?' he called again as he pushed himself further out onto the collapsed building. 'Can you still hear me?

'Yes.'

The voice was faint and raspy but it was real. And it was female.

She was real and she was alive!

Excitement rushed through his body, flooding his muscles with adrenalin. Finally, they could mark another name off the list and this time they had a survivor.

'Can you tell me your name?'

'Charlotte. Charlotte Lawson.'

Could it be?

'Charli? Is that you? It's Patrick.'

'Patrick?'

'I've been looking for you.' He couldn't believe he had found her, that she was alive. It was a miracle. But he didn't believe in miracles. 'Are you hurt?'

'No. Not badly. But my sister, Amy… I don't know where she is. It's pitch-black in here, I can't see anything. The walls have collapsed and I'm trapped. Please, help us.'

'Charli, Amy is okay. She wasn't in the building.'

'Are you sure?'

'Positive. I've seen her. I've spoken to her. I'll get her here and you can talk to her.' He could hear Charli sobbing with relief.

'Don't leave me.'

'I won't leave you. I promise. I'm going to get you out but you need to listen to me. It's going to take time but I give you my word we will get you out.' He did his best to sound reassuring but he had heard the wobble in her voice. He could only imagine what she was thinking, how she was feeling. It was a miracle that she'd been found and that she was, apparently, unharmed, but Pat knew they'd need another miracle to get her out before anything untoward happened.

There had been other casualties who had survived the landslide only to perish before they'd been able to rescue them, and those deaths weighed heavily on his conscience. He'd talked to those people but hadn't been able to save them. He wasn't going to let the same fate befall Charli.

He turned back to Connor and saw he already had his radio in his hand and was putting the call out. Within seconds their team was reassembling, along with the medical specialists and engineers who had been flown in to Wombat Gully. The chapel bells were ringing again and the noise level intensified as people poured out, buzzing with excitement as the news spread.

A survivor!

Pat could hear Connor briefing the teams. The site had been cordoned off but he knew that once news broke that a survivor had been located, the media would be pressing in as close as possible. Connor was issuing instructions to the police to expand the cordon to give them more privacy. They needed to be able to communicate with Charli and extraneous noise wasn't going to be helpful.

Pat was handed a headset and a search cam, a thin, flexible pole with a camera on the end that could be fed through small gaps. 'All right, Charli. We're going to send a camera down to you. It'll have a light on it and a microphone. I'll be wearing a headset so you can talk to me. I'll be listening.'

A hole needed to be drilled through the concrete in order to feed the camera through. The engineer tried to convince Pat to leave while he worked, worried about the slab taking their combined weight. 'No. I'm staying,' Pat argued. 'Connor and I were both on the slab and it held. I need to be here.'

'Charli.' He spoke to her, letting her know their plans. 'We need to drill a small hole to get the camera through. It's going to get noisy for a few minutes but I'll still be right here.'

The engineer used a diamond-tipped drill and made a small opening. Pat pushed the pole into the gap but the camera showed nothing. There was a small space but it was empty. There was no one in it.

Disappointment and frustration flooded

through him. He'd been sure they were in the right place.

Pat spoke over his shoulder to the site engineer. 'How many apartments were in this building?'

'Twelve, four floors, three on each floor. You should be right above her.'

Pat checked the surroundings. Was there another floor under this slab? There didn't look as though there was enough space. The concrete slab they had drilled through and the space he was looking at through the camera must only be a few feet off the ground. Where was she?

'She's got to be here. There must be a second slab. We'll have to go through the next one.' That had to be the only solution.

The engineer nodded and issued directives to Pat to pass on to Charli.

'Charli, I think we're right above you. We're going to drill carefully through more concrete. It could be close to you. We'll go slowly and stop regularly to check in with you. I need you to tell us if you're worried about anything.'

'How will I know? I can't see.'

Pat knew that was a problem. They had to

be careful and had no way of knowing where she was. They could be drilling right above her head. 'Charli, are you sitting up or lying down?' he asked.

'I'm lying down, there's not much room here.'

They needed more information. 'Can you reach your hand above your head? How much space is there?'

'Maybe a foot.'

'What about around you?'

'I'm on the bed. There's a wall to my left and maybe a few feet to my right and at the foot of the bed. I think the frame of the bed head is holding up the ceiling.'

'Okay. That's great, Charli, you're doing well.'

He couldn't continue the conversation while the engineers were drilling but they stopped every couple of minutes, giving him an opportunity to check in.

'How are you doing, Charli?'

'I'm okay. Cold and thirsty.'

'I'll buy you a hot chocolate when we get you out of here.'

'Is that a promise?'

'For sure.' He should have insisted on buying her a drink on Friday night. Maybe then she would have still been in the bar when the landslide had occurred. Maybe then she would have been safe. He knew he couldn't keep everyone safe but he wished he'd followed his heart. He promised himself he wouldn't take the safe option next time. 'You must be hungry too.'

'I am. How long have I been stuck in here?'

'About thirty-six hours.'

'*What?* What day is it?' she asked.

'Sunday.'

'*Sunday!* What time is it?'

'Almost eleven in the morning.'

It had been nearly four hours since he'd come on shift. He wondered if he'd be made to leave when his shift ended. He knew that protocol dictated that he should, but he also knew he would argue against it. There was no way he was leaving the site until they'd got Charli out of there.

'Okay, I think we're almost there,' he said. 'The drilling's going to start again.'

Another couple of minutes was all that was needed before the engineer gave Pat a thumbs-up.

'I can see a tiny bit of light!' Charli's voice carried up to him.

They were through.

Pat fed the search cam through the next layer of concrete. When it emerged into the next space he could see a figure curled on a bed. They'd done it!

She was hugging her knees to her chest and she looked cold and vulnerable, but they'd found her and she was alive.

She was looking up into the camera and Pat barely recognised her. In the bar he'd been completely blind-sided by her beauty. She'd had the kind of face that stopped men in the street, a perfect oval framed by thick blonde hair, she'd had flawless skin and enormous blue eyes, but now her hair was matted and filthy, her face smeared with mud, and he could see a darker stain on the left side of her forehead. A bruise. Or maybe blood. Her eyes were pale and huge in her face and she looked terrified. He wanted desperately to get in there to comfort her. She looked as though she needed it.

Everything was covered with mud. Including Charli. The space was a mess, the bed was buckled and Pat could see a crushed wardrobe and what was possibly the remains of a bedside table. A lamp lay on the floor in the mud.

Charli was looking around and Pat wondered if the light was a mistake. Was it giving her more of an idea about the predicament she was in? Would seeing her surroundings add to the trauma?

'Hey, there.' Pat spoke through the microphone. 'Can you hear me clearly?'

Charli turned her head back towards the camera. She couldn't see him but it was obviously an instinctive move to turn towards the sound.

'Yes.' She nodded. 'Can you get me out now?'

'Can't wait for that hot chocolate, hey?'

'I'm cold.'

She gave him a half-smile and his spirits lifted. She was tough. He knew she'd pull through but he vowed to be there to help her. 'We'll get you out as soon as we can.'

Retrieving her was going to be a slow process but Pat was feeling truly positive for the first time since the disaster.

'Is Amy there? Can I talk to her?'

'Yes, of course.' He'd seen Amy arrive on

the scene. Someone had tracked her down. 'Amy can't come onto the site but I'll take my headset to her. Give me a moment.'

He found Amy and passed the headset to her. It was probably a good idea to let her talk to her sister. While he didn't want to think about the worst-case scenario there was no denying this whole exercise was risky and Pat knew it could go horribly wrong. He wasn't going to deny the siblings the opportunity to talk. Who knew what could happen next?

Amy had tears streaming down her face as she put the headset on. 'I'm sorry, Charli. I should have come home with you.'

He could only hear one side of the conversation but it was enough to give him the gist of it.

'But at least we would have been together.

'Are you hurt?

'You're sure?

'I know. Okay. I'll be waiting for you. I love you.'

Amy removed the headset and passed it back to Pat. 'Promise me you'll get her out,' she pleaded. 'She's the only family I've got.'

'I promise,' he said as he signalled to one of his team members to swap places with him as he spoke again to Charli. 'The engineers are going to continue to enlarge this opening and I'm going to hand over the communication to Dave, who's also a paramedic, while I see what I can do about getting you warmed up.' He knew she would be frozen. Everything looked wet or at least damp and there had been no heating. 'Is that okay?'

'Will you be back?'

'Before you know it.'

Pat switched places with Dave. He wanted to have a discussion with Melissa Cartwright, the ED doctor who had been choppered in to Wombat Gully to co-ordinate any medical care. They needed a plan. A triage and stabilising centre had been set up in the resort medical centre but the first step before they could treat Charli was getting her out of there safely.

'How do you think she's doing?' Melissa asked.

'She seems lucid. No significant injuries. Cold and thirsty.' Pat summarised what he knew so far. 'It's going to be a tricky extraction. There are two slabs of concrete above her and the engineers don't think we can get in underneath without the risk of the whole structure collapsing. We'll have to go through the slabs. It's going to take time.'

'Hypothermia is a risk,' Melissa said. 'We need to warm her up, get fluids into her, and we need to be able to monitor her condition.'

'Okay, we'll get some leads through as soon as possible.' He turned to Connor. 'Can you organise a bear-hugger?'

He waited for confirmation before he crawled back out onto the slab. He tapped Dave on the shoulder and slipped the headset back on, restoring communication with Charli.

'Hey, there, Charli, it's Pat. I'm back.'

Charli closed her eyes at the sound of Pat's voice. Dave had tried to have a conversation with her but she didn't have the energy to start over. She only had enough energy for Pat and she could feel herself relax now that he was back. She'd been edgy when he'd left. Even though another paramedic had taken his place she'd felt as though she'd lost the lifeline that tethered her to the world above. The world outside her tomb. She took a deep breath and opened her eyes.

'You still doing okay?' he asked.

His voice was deep and mellow and sooth-
ing. He sounded in control and that calmed
her nerves. His voice made her feel safe.

She pictured his face, his smile that had
made his eyes crinkle at the corners, the little scar under his left eye, and his messy,
dark hair. She remembered the warmth of
his hands on her elbows and wished he was
with her now. She longed for some warmth
and she longed for the touch of another person. More specifically, she found herself
longing for him.

'I'm good,' she replied, which was a ridiculous thing to say given she was buried under
tonnes of rubble. But at least she was alive.
'But I'll be better when you get me out of
here.' She knew he'd get her out. She trusted
him.

'That's the way.' She could hear the smile
in his voice and knowing she'd made him
smile lifted her spirits. 'All right, the engineers have made a hole large enough through
both slabs that I can start passing some things
down to you.'

The hole was above her chest. She could
see light coming in but she couldn't see out.
She wriggled around on the bed so her face

was underneath the hole. She could see blue sky. She winced and closed her eyes. The sky was far too bright after hours of darkness but she couldn't resist slowly opening them once more because she had wondered if she'd ever see the sky again.

The sunlight dimmed as Pat's face appeared in the hole, illuminated from below by the small light on the search cam.

'Hello again.'

She smiled at the sight of him, pleased that his face was the first she would see. His dark hair was sticking out in all directions, wild and unruly. His jaw was covered in dark stubble and he was smiling at her, his teeth white against the darkness of his beard. His eyes crinkled at the corners and she was struck by the life in them and by their colour.

'Your eyes are green!'

'You do remember me, don't you?' he teased her, and she felt herself smiling properly in return. She hadn't thought she'd ever feel like smiling again.

'Yes, of course, but in the bar I thought your eyes were brown.'

His face disappeared all too suddenly. She wanted to call out and ask him to come back. She wanted to keep looking at him. She wanted one last chance to burn his face into her memory just in case things went wrong. But she was too slow. His face was gone from sight and her heart plunged in her chest. It was a stupid thing to be disappointed about as she knew, given her situation, that there were more important things for her to think about, but she really liked his face.

His hand was reaching down through the hole. The hole was small and it was a tight fit. His forearm filled the space. He could almost touch her. He was still within reach. All she had to do was lift her hand and she would have that connection. She reached up and held onto his fingers. He wasn't wearing gloves and his hand was warm. Hers was freezing by comparison. He must have just removed his glove and she was grateful. She craved warmth. Her body craved the touch of another person. She remembered how she'd felt when he'd held her before. Twice he'd caught her, supported her and made her safe. She wished he was there with her now. Tears sprang to her eyes and she wiped them from her face with her other hand, pleased he couldn't see her reaction through the tiny gap that his arm had filled.

'Hey, what's wrong?'

His voice came through the microphone. She'd forgotten about the tiny camera that had been fed into her space. She could see the thin pole running along the length of his arm. Just because she couldn't see him didn't mean he couldn't see her.

'I wasn't sure I'd ever see another person again,' she answered honestly.

She held onto his hand for several seconds before letting go. She didn't want to let go, she felt safe with her hand in his, but she wanted to see his face again. She needed to see his smile.

He removed his arm and suddenly there he was, grinning down at her again.

'Sorry, it was my face you got.'

'I'm glad it's you. You have a very nice face.'

She wondered what had got into her. She never volunteered her feelings. She'd learnt to bottle them up since her mother had died. Showing your feelings gave other people a chance to hurt you, but for the first time in hours her fears were receding and it was all to do with this man.

'Are you positive you're not injured? Concussion, perhaps?' He was still grinning at her.

'I might have a slight concussion,' she admitted, and then she smiled. 'And my eyes might need a bit more time to get accustomed to the light.' A little levity made her feel much better. Much more positive.

'That would explain it. I'll make a note to get your eyes tested when we get you out of there.'

'You will get me out, won't you?'

'We will. This is what we've been hoping for. *You're* what we've been hoping for.'

'What do you mean?' She saw a little crease appear between his dark eyebrows. There was a worried look in his green eyes and Charli felt a flutter of panic. 'What is it? What's wrong?'

'We've been searching for two days. You're the first person we've found.'

'The first person? Are other people missing?' For some reason she'd imagined that whatever had gone wrong had only affected her apartment. She hadn't considered other people for one minute. She hadn't had room in her head for those thoughts but now she really needed to know what was going on. 'What happened?'

'There was a landslide. It started on the mountain above you.' He paused and she sensed he was figuring out how much to tell her. How bad could it be? 'Two lodges collapsed and sixteen people were missing.'

'Sixteen! How many have you found?'

'Ten. Including you.'

She knew she should be grateful that she'd been found but she was struggling with the horror of the situation. It was hard to wrap her head around. A landslide. Whole buildings collapsed. Six people still missing. She was too scared to ask how many others had survived.

'All right, time to get to work.' Pat's voice jolted her back to the present. 'We have a team of people up here—Dave you've met, Dr Melissa Cartwright, an ED specialist, engineers, mining experts and lots of pairs of hands all working to get you out, but first we need to check your condition. I'm going to start sending a few things your way. We're going to pump some warm air in and also set up a tube with some warm fluids to rehydrate you, but I'll also send down an oxygen mask and some leads to monitor your condition. Obviously, I can't get down to you yet but I'll talk you through it all.'

'I know what to do.'

'You do?'

'I'm a doctor.'

'You're a doctor?'

'Yes. I've just finished my Foundation Training. I'm about to start GP training.' She couldn't remember if she'd told him that. She couldn't have.

'That'll make things easier,' he said as he passed a thermometer down through the hole. 'Are you able to take an axillary temp for me?'

'Yes.' She was willing to do just about anything for him at this point in time.

She reached up for the thermometer, preparing herself for his touch this time, telling herself not to hold onto him, but her loneliness, fear and despair were still so close to the surface of her emotions that the touch of his hand brought tears to her eyes once again. The warmth of his fingers set her nerves alight, sending sparks shooting up her arm.

She would have thought it was just because of the contrast in temperature between his skin and hers except for the fact that his touch set her heart racing. She fought to control her breathing, to control her heart rate, knowing she needed to stay calm, but it was difficult when all she wanted to do was cling to Pat and never let go.

Deciding she'd have to figure out how to cope with his touch, she put the thermometer under her armpit and clamped it in place. She didn't want to send them all into a panic when her pulse was taken.

She passed the thermometer back up through the hole, disappointed when Pat held it by the end, meaning she missed his touch. She could hear them discussing the reading. She knew her temperature was low as she'd read the numbers before passing it back. It was thirty-three point five degrees, and even though an axillary reading could be a degree out it was still well below a normal temperature of thirty-six point eight. But she was reassured by the fact that, despite the quilt, she was still shivering. That was potentially a good sign. She was possibly only mildly hypothermic.

Pat's hand appeared through the hole once more as he passed down some warmed blankets, some chemical heat packs, an oxygen mask and a pulse oximeter.

As she looked at the assortment it hit home that, as Pat had told her, it would take a while to get her out of there. She wrapped the blankets around her and then tucked the heat packs underneath. Fortunately Pat had already broken them to start the chemical reaction as she doubted she'd have the strength or dexterity in her cold, stiff fingers to do it herself. She bent her knees to hold one in her groin and another against her stomach. She'd love a pair of socks for her frozen feet but she knew the dangers of warming her extremities up too quickly. Forcing cold blood away from her hands and feet and back to her heart was highly risky and could be fatal.

Next through the hole was a long plastic feeding tube. Pat's voice came through the microphone. 'This is warm fluid, sip it slowly.'

She clipped the pulse oximeter onto her forefinger and sipped on the electrolyte and nutrient mixture. She thought it was possibly the best thing she'd tasted, ever. She took a couple of sips and then put the oxygen mask on.

'Keep the tube close,' Pat told her. 'Take a couple of mouthfuls at regular intervals, I'll tell you when. And one more thing, I'm going to pass a pipe down through the hole. It's called a bear-hugger and it looks like a vacuum-cleaner hose, but it's basically a heater. We'll blow warm air into your space and slowly increase the temperature. You're not going to be able to see out through this hole any more and the engineers are going to start drilling to my right, above your feet. Okay?'

Charli nodded. She closed her eyes and held the kindness in his eyes and the warmth of his smile in her heart.

She flinched as the engineers began drilling again. The noise startled her and the vibrations rattled and shook her surroundings, just like during the landslide. It was frightening. She tried to slow her breathing, knowing her respirations and heart rate were being monitored for signs of stress, but she knew she was failing. She could hear herself sucking in lungfuls of oxygen through the mask. But at least it went some way towards blocking out the smell of diesel fuel, sewage and mud.

Finally the noise ground to a halt and she felt herself relax. She opened her eyes. Had they made it through already? That hadn't been too bad.

But she saw no difference in her surroundings. A hole had not miraculously opened up at her feet. She was still entombed.

'How're you doing, Charli?'

'It sounds as though the ceiling is going to collapse.' She found it difficult to talk, her accelerated heartbeat making her breathing shallow.

'I promise we know what we're doing. Would you like to listen to some music? That might block out some of the noise. Who do you like to listen to?'

'Adele.'

'Who?'

'Adele. She's an English singer. You haven't heard of her?' Charli could feel her breathing and heart-rate return to normal as Pat's voice calmed her down. If only he could be in her tiny space with her, she knew she'd feel better. She thought she could cope with anything if he was beside her. 'I thought she was big all round the world.'

'She probably is. I spend most of my time listening to *The Wiggles*.'

Charli had vaguely heard of *The Wiggles*. She thought they were a children's music group. 'You have kids?'

'A daughter. She's three.'

Of course he had a family. Disappointment flooded through her. She hadn't realised she'd been building a whole fantasy world for him to exist in, and it hadn't included a wife and family. She closed her eyes and sighed. He hadn't been wearing a wedding ring but that didn't mean he didn't have a partner. But if that were the case, why had he offered to buy her a drink and take her to brunch? She knew the answer to that one. Because all men were bastards. She certainly knew how to pick them. Or did they pick her? Was there something about her that attracted unfaithful men?

'Charli? Are you still with me?'

CHAPTER FIVE

'CHARLI? CAN YOU still hear me?'

Pat watched her through the monitor, his heart racing as panic gripped him. Her eyes were closed, dark eyelashes resting against pale cheeks. Was she conscious? Hypothermic? Was she all right? He couldn't see if her chest was moving and his concern escalated as the silence stretched on.

'Charli?'

'Are you married?'

He breathed out a sigh of relief as Charli opened her eyes and spoke to him. He hadn't realised he'd been holding his breath, anxiously waiting to hear her voice.

'What?' It took him a second or two to process her question. 'No, I'm not married.'

Margie had been dead for two years. He'd come to terms with the fact that she was gone but even though he still thought of her as his wife he didn't think of himself as married. He was very much alone.

'But you have a daughter?'

'Yes.' Alone except for Ella.

'Where is she?'

'In Melbourne.'

'Do you live in Melbourne?'

'Yes.'

'You were supposed to have left Wombat Gully by now, weren't you? You told me you were going to Melbourne on the night we met.'

'Yes. The landslide changed my plans somewhat.'

'It's lucky for me that you're here, though. I don't suppose anyone expected a real drill. Have you trained for this?'

'Are you asking to check my references? I promise I know what I'm doing. I've been a paramedic for ten years and part of the Special Operations team for five.'

'Is your Special Operations involved in rescues like our Hazardous Area Response Teams? You said you jump out of helicopters and abseil down mountains?'

'We don't do that every day.' He smiled. 'But, yes, it's the same as your HART teams.'

'How did you get into that?'

'These mountains are my back yard. I grew up less than an hour from here and spent all my spare time skiing, mountain biking, rock climbing and generally getting into trouble that I had to get myself out of. I joined the ambulance service and it was a natural progression to Special Ops for me. Did you get to work with the HART teams while you were studying medicine?'

'No,' she said. 'I'm not sure that I'm an emergency medicine type of girl. I like to play it safe. Amy is the adventurous sister.'

'Is she a professional ski instructor?' He wanted to keep her talking. Wanted to make sure she stayed conscious and alert, and if she wasn't going to listen to music then talking to him might help keep her mind off the extraction process.

'Amy trained as a primary teacher but she hasn't spent a lot of time teaching. She spends most of her time travelling, working around the world. She always does kids' ski school lessons so I guess she is using her teaching degree. She's done a bit of teaching in developing countries but I think she likes the freedom of the ski fields. This is her third winter here.'

'But your first visit? We're not giving you a very good impression, are we?'

'I'll admit it's been a bit more dramatic than I like my holidays to be.'

They were an hour into the process when Pat's stomach started to grumble. It was time for another break in the drilling and he hoped no one else heard the rumbling. He knew he was overdue for a break but he wasn't going to leave Charli. She wasn't having anything more than warmed fluids and he felt it would be unfair of him to be too comfortable. Why should he get to have a full stomach, toilet breaks and showers? He wanted to feel what Charli was feeling and keeping a level of discomfort allowed him to do that.

He wanted to stay close by, wanted to be able to talk to her. It was about more than just keeping her calm. He wanted to be the one who was there for her, wanted to be the one to talk to her in the five-minute break between drilling. Having built up rapport and trust, he didn't want anyone else taking over. He suspected their conversation was as important to him as it was to her. Despite the circumstances, their conversation flowed easily. He couldn't remember feeling so comfortable with someone who was a virtual stranger. The dates he'd been on in the past two years had mostly been dreadful. Awkward and difficult. But there was no awkwardness with Charli.

The situation lent itself to honesty. If she asked him a question he felt obliged to give her an honest answer. Perhaps it helped her that she couldn't see him. Maybe it was a bit like being in a confessional box or being given the last rites. He wasn't religious, not at all, but he thought there was probably something to be said for being able to get things off your chest, admitting to your sins and so on. Not that he was prepared to entertain the idea that Charli might not survive this. He wasn't going to be the last person she spoke to or the last person she saw, but he could be the person she talked to at this moment in her life. He could be the one who helped her.

'Charli, did you want me to see if there's any mobile phone service? Maybe put a call in to your parents?' Charli had spoken to Amy but he was sure she'd like a chance to speak to her parents. They'd managed to keep her identity from the media. Amy wasn't speaking to the journalists but Pat knew the disastrous event was getting global coverage.

'No, there's no one I need to speak to.'

'We haven't released your name yet but, at some point your name will hit the headlines. It might be wise to give your parents a heads-up. Perhaps Amy could call them and break the news and then you could speak to them? You don't want to speak to your mother?'

'My mother is dead.'

Too late he remembered that Amy had told him Charli was her only family. *Way to go, Pat, great choice of topic.* Maybe he should let Charli ask the questions, that way he wouldn't be hearing answers he wasn't expecting and didn't know how to react to.

'I'm sorry to hear that,' he said.

Through the search cam he could see Charli shrug her shoulders. 'It was a long time ago,' she said. 'It's been me and Amy, just the two of us, for almost as long as I can remember.'

'Is your father alive?'

'Yes. But I don't need to talk to him. I don't think he even knows where we are. He won't miss either of us.'

Pat frowned. That seemed like an odd thing to say. Why wouldn't he know, or care, where his daughters were? If Ella was in trouble halfway around the world, he knew he'd want to know. But he would save his questions for another time as he sensed he wasn't going to lighten the mood any by delving further.

'There's no one else?'

'No.'

Surely she had someone? Pat didn't understand. Everyone had somebody, didn't they? He had his parents and a younger brother, he'd had Margie and now he had Ella. He'd never had no one.

'Just Amy.'

Her voice was quiet but he realised as she spoke that of course she had someone. Amy was her someone. That was okay. He'd talk to her about Amy, that would keep her mind occupied while they worked to get her out.

'So, you're here on holiday but Amy is working here?' He had learned that Snowgum Chalet was used as accommodation for Wombat Gully resort staff.

'Yes. I came on a bit of a whim. She's been telling me for years how fabulous Australia is—I'm not sure that I believe her given the situation I'm in, but anyway I needed to see her, so here I am.'

'Why did you need to see her?'

'I had a fight with my boyfriend.'

'It's a long way to come after a fight.'

'It was a big one.' He heard the smile in her voice and saw the corners of her mouth lift. That was better, she had a much more positive tone.

'Big enough that you don't want to call him? Let him know what's happened?'

'He's now my ex. I don't want to call him,' she said with a shake of her head. 'He doesn't deserve to know what has happened. I don't want to talk to him, see him, have anything to do with him. That's one thing I'm sure of after all this time in here. I've had plenty of time to think about what really matters to me. And he isn't on my list.'

'That sounds like a doozy of a fight.'

'It was.'

'Do you want to talk about it?'

'I haven't told anyone about this except for Amy.' He thought that was the end of it but then she continued. 'I was in Spain with a girlfriend. We were celebrating the end of our Foundation training when Jane's father had a stroke. Jane wanted to fly back to the UK so I went with her. When I walked into my flat I found my boyfriend in bed with another girl. I don't know who was more surprised, Hugo, her or me.'

Pat wasn't sure if she was laughing or crying.

'I couldn't stay there and I was too shocked to think about kicking him out so I fled. I was still on holiday before I start the next stage of my training, so I came here. For almost as long as I can remember Amy has been the one I've run to when things haven't worked out.'

'Do you want to work things out with him?'

'Are you kidding?' Her voice regained some strength and volume. 'I'd never be able to trust him again. And he was either unhappy in the relationship or less invested in it than I was or just a complete arse.'

Pat was surprised how pleased he was to hear that Charli was definitely single. He was also pleased to hear some fire in her voice and to see a spark return to her eyes. There was still some fight left in her and he knew she was going to need it.

The next time the drilling stopped Charli tried to steer the conversation towards Pat. She was tired of talking about her life, nothing in it was going according to plan and she'd rather forget about it for a while. She didn't have a high opinion of men at this point in time but Pat seemed like he might be one of the good guys. The world could do with more men like him. *She* could do with a man like him.

'Tell me something more about you,' she said to him the next chance she got. 'How did you get that scar under your eye?'

'That's what you want to know?'

'Mmm-hmm, I've been wondering about it since I first saw you.'

'Is that a fact? And here I was, thinking that in your jet-lagged state, you'd barely re-membered me.'

She still couldn't see him but she could hear the smile in his voice. She wished she could see it again but just thinking about his smile was enough to lift her mood. 'I remem-bered you. So, how did you get the scar? Were you rescuing someone else or doing some-thing dangerous?'

'None of the above. Doing something stu-pid, more like it. My brother and I were prac-tising our whip-cracking skills. I was holding a stick in my mouth and he was trying to crack it out. Needless to say, he missed the stick and got me under the eye. Our mother confiscated the whip and we were grounded for weeks.'

He was laughing and she'd bet he and his brother had given their mother plenty to worry about. 'Are you and your brother close?' It sounded as if they were.

'Yeah, we are.'

Lost in her thoughts, it took her a moment to realise that everything had gone silent above her. Immediately she thought the worst. 'Pat? Are you still there? Is something wrong?'

'No, everything's great.' His voice came down to her, reassuring and calm. 'The engineers are just about to remove the final piece of concrete. It's time to get you out.'

'Really?'

She started to sit up, forgetting once again that he could see her.

'Don't move! We need to take this slowly.'

Charli put her head down and watched as a backpack was lowered to the floor through the hole that the engineers had made at the foot of her bed. The bag was followed by a pair of boots and then legs in bright red trousers appeared followed by a body in a jacket and, finally, Patrick's head and face emerged.

He had a hard hat on with a bright light shining out from the front straight into her eyes.

She winced and he angled the light up. 'Sorry,' he said as he squatted on the floor and looked around.

'Don't apologise. I don't think I've ever been as glad to see another person in my life.'

He grinned.

She couldn't believe that he was there, that she wasn't alone any more.

She couldn't take her eyes off him. Her knight in rescue gear. He was tall and muscular and broad shouldered and took up a lot of the minimal space but she didn't mind. She was more than happy to share her space. Finally she could let herself believe she was going to get out of there.

Tears threatened as she realised she was actually going to make it out alive.

'Hey, it's all right, you're okay. Everything's going to be okay.' He was beside her now, his voice confident and reassuring as he leant over her and gathered her into his arms. She didn't think she'd ever felt anything as wonderful as his embrace. After more than forty hours trapped and alone, to have someone close enough to touch, close enough to feel the warmth of his breath on her cheek, was overwhelming. 'We'll do this together, okay?'

She nodded. 'Okay.'

'We're going to take it slow.'

'I just want to get out of here.'

'I know you do and don't worry, that's the next thing on my list, but we don't want to move you too quickly. Trust me.'

Charli knew there had been cases of hypothermic patients suffering cardiac arrest caused by toxins in the bloodstream. He was right to go slowly, she didn't want to have survived this long only to encounter another trauma. She bit back her impatience and chose to follow his instructions. He'd got her safely to this point. She chose to trust him.

He was still holding her hand and his dark green eyes didn't leave her face as he waited for her to agree.

She nodded.

He let go of her and reached for the backpack, dragging it towards him. The backpack contained a medical kit and he searched through it, pulling out a small torch.

'Close your eyes,' he told her.

She did as he instructed and waited for him to lift her eyelids as he shone the torch in her eyes. The light was bright and she was certain her pupils contracted in response but his expression gave nothing away. He was thorough and gentle as he checked her injuries. He unwrapped her makeshift bandages from her leg and hand and rinsed the wound on her leg with saline before quickly rewrapping her calf with clean dressings. His hands were warm and gentle. She closed her eyes and held her breath as he held her calf.

'Am I hurting you?' he asked.

She opened her eyes and shook her head. She had no pain but his touch was doing funny things to her insides. Making her quiver.

He wrapped another blanket around her shoulders.

She should tell him she wasn't shaking from cold but she couldn't speak.

She lay still and silent as he cleaned and checked and re-dressed the wound on the palm of her hand. She was aware of how filthy she was. Her hair was matted and she was covered in mud and blood and who knew what else after being entombed for hours. She wished she was cleaner, wished she smelt better, wished she could have a warm bath, but all of that would have to wait.

She flinched when she felt a sting in her elbow.

'Sorry,' he said as he inserted a bung. 'I want to get that in now so we can attach a drip and get you straight into the ambulance. There are a lot of news crews up above and we really don't want to treat you in full view of them.'

He brushed her hair from her forehead. Their faces were close. Close enough that she could see the individual hairs in the stubble of his beard. Close enough that she could feel his breath on her cheek. Close enough that she could press her lips to his if she chose.

She closed her eyes again as she imagined his lips brushing over hers. Imagined him leaning in to kiss her, even though she knew he was only inspecting the cut on her forehead.

She flinched as he rinsed the wound with saline and she reminded herself that he was taking care of her because that was his job. Kissing her would be the last thing on his mind. 'We'll do it properly up above but that will do for now,' he told her, before calling out to the crew above them.

Charli watched as a spinal board and harness were lowered through the hole. Pat undid the straps and laid the board beside her. 'I'm going to harness you to the spinal board to take you out.'

His arms encircled her as he slid the harness straps under her chest. They were pressed almost cheek to cheek in the confined space and she wanted desperately to burrow into his embrace.

'I'm going to roll you onto the board now.'

He rolled her away from him and she felt the hard edge of the spinal board against her back. She could feel the warmth of his hands through the thin latex of the surgical gloves that covered his fingers as he rolled her back onto the board. In contrast to his fingers the board was cold and uncomfortable under her spine.

'Slowly straighten your legs.'

Her legs were stiff and her knees felt locked.

'Take your time.' He waited until she was

able to lie flat. He reached up and clipped two carabiners to her harness and the spinal board before covering her legs with a blanket. 'Okay, here we go.'

He called out to the team of people on the surface, 'Ready!'

And Charli felt herself being lifted out.

Pat was left below her and she almost wished she was still there with him. She wasn't ready to leave him.

Her stretcher was put on the ground and she was surrounded by the rescue crew. She was in the centre of a circle, shielded from view as people double-checked her vital signs.

A woman leaned over her, introducing herself as the ED doctor, Melissa, but Charli wasn't registering much more than that. She was looking for Pat.

She heard someone comment on her heart rate and her respirations. She was aware that her breathing was fast and that her heart rate had accelerated. She knew it was important to stay calm but she needed to see Pat. She needed him to tether her, to slow her panic, to make her feel safe, even now that she was out.

And then she saw him. He'd followed her straight out of the hole. She could see his unruly dark hair as his head emerged from the rubble, half-hidden behind the rest of the people, but it wasn't until he was kneeling beside her, until she felt the weight of his hand on her arm, that she could breathe normally again.

'Look at me, Charli, breathe with me,' he said. 'You're okay…everything is going to be okay.'

Again, he held her gaze, watching and waiting for her to calm down. Again, she had the sense that she could trust him. That he wouldn't leave her.

'Look at the sky,' he said as she got her breathing under control.

She looked past him now, over his shoulder.

The sun was beginning to set and the sky was streaked with pink and orange. It looked like someone had pulled swathes of fairy floss across the sky. The mountain across the valley was covered in snow and the sunset was turning it pink. There was no wind, the air was still.

'It's beautiful,' she whispered, scarcely able to believe she was actually out and able to see the sky.

She was aware of cheers now and of a flurry of flashes and bright lights. Pat had

warned her that the media had been covering the situation twenty-four seven, reporting
on the bad news and hoping for some good.

'They've been waiting a long time for this
moment. You'll be the headline on the evening news.'

She'd known they would film her extraction but she didn't care. She brought her
eyes back to Pat. He was all she could see.
All she *wanted* to see. In the evening light
she could see that his dark green eyes had a
lighter hazel ring around the edge. His smile
was white and his jaw was darkened by that
five-o'clock shadow. She couldn't remember
if he'd started the day with stubble. Was it
designer or was it just because of his dark
colouring?

'On the count of three,' she heard someone
say. 'One, two, three.'

She felt her stretcher being lifted. Pat took
one side, next to her head. She didn't look
to see who the other stretcher bearers were.
Charli kept her eyes on Pat as she was carried
across the rubble. She saw the open doors of
an ambulance and felt herself being lowered
onto the ambulance stretcher.

She saw Pat let go of her and her heart missed a beat as panic rose in her chest.

'Are you coming with me?' she asked.

'Don't you want Amy to go with you?'

'Can't you both come?'

He shook his head and her heart plummeted.

'Do you have to go back out there?' she asked. He'd spent hours with her, talking to her, comforting her, helping her through the process. She wondered how he coped with the pressure and couldn't imagine how he would be able to go back and do it all over again.

'No. My shift is finished, I'm due a break,' he said, 'but there's not enough room in the ambulance for Amy and me. I'll meet you at the medical centre.'

CHAPTER SIX

'OKAY,' CHARLI REPLIED just as Amy was ushered through the crowd of medics and rescue workers. Her face was tearstained but she was smiling. She leant over and hugged Charli, somehow managing not to dislodge the myriad tubes and monitor leads that the paramedics had already attached to her.

'Charli, thank God,' she sobbed. 'I thought I'd lost you.'

Amy's voice was thick with emotion and Charli fought back tears of her own as she hugged her sister. She'd had exactly the same thoughts while she'd been buried alive before Pat had put her mind at ease. 'Are you going to be okay?' Amy asked as she released her.

'I'll be fine,' she replied as she was loaded into the ambulance. Amy climbed into the back too and knelt beside her.

Charli flinched as the doors were slammed

shut and Patrick disappeared from her view. She wasn't ready to say goodbye. He'd got her through her ordeal, he'd been with her every step, and she needed him.

She lifted one hand in a silent farewell. 'What do you need?' Amy asked her, misinterpreting her gesture.

'Nothing.' Amy would never understand if Charli asked for Pat to accompany her in the ambulance instead. She couldn't do that to her sister. She was still the most important person in her life. Amy was still her someone.

Charli closed her eyes as it was easier to pretend to be tired than to talk. Not that she was pretending. She was exhausted, emotionally and physically drained, and she missed Pat's calming presence already. When she'd been trapped she'd wanted her sister. Now Amy was beside her and she wanted Pat, but she knew she couldn't put that longing into words without hurting Amy. So she kept her eyes closed and her mouth shut. It was fortunate that no one seemed to expect much more from her.

Amy held her hand while the ambulance drove slowly through the resort but Charli only opened her eyes when the ambulance stopped moving. The journey lasted only a few minutes before her stretcher was unloaded and she was wheeled into the resort medical centre. Screens had been erected to block the inquisitive journalists and news cameras but they worked both ways, Charli realised, as they prevented her from seeing if Patrick had followed her, as he'd promised. She was pushed into a treatment room but not moved from the stretcher.

The doctor was already there. Charli thought her name was Melissa, and she heard her issue instructions to the other staff who darted in and out of the room. She gave up trying to keep track of all the comings and goings—the movements combined with the bright fluorescent lights overhead were starting to give her a headache. She turned her head and looked at Amy, who still hadn't let go of her hand, as the medical staff poked and prodded her and discussed her condition—which they announced was surprisingly good—and her injuries—relatively minor considering everything that had happened. She had three frostbitten toes, a cut to her head and two further cuts, one on her hand and another on her calf, that would need stitching.

'I'm going to attach a drip and start a course of antibiotics,' Melissa told Charli. 'And then I'll clean and suture your wounds.'

Charli could feel her heart rate and respiration rate accelerating and she watched the numbers rise on the monitor, which was completely counterproductive and just made the numbers rise more rapidly.

Melissa glanced at the monitor. 'Amy, would you mind waiting outside for a minute?'

The treatment process wasn't bothering Charli but she didn't mention that it wasn't the idea of stitches that was making her nervous. She was wondering where Pat was. He'd said he'd meet her there and she wondered if he was waiting outside. Being without him was making her anxious.

A sharp prick in her leg drew her attention back to the room and to what was going on around her. She looked down at her leg. Melissa had injected a local anaesthetic into her calf and was about to start cleaning and stitching her wound. She moved onto Charli's hand next and once her hand and leg were numb she became aware of pain in her feet. She wriggled in the bed, trying to find a comfortable position, but the pain didn't abate.

Melissa looked up at her. 'What's the matter, Charli? I need you to stay still.'

'My feet.' Charli gritted her teeth as she tried to ignore the pain long enough to speak. She didn't think she'd ever been in as much pain as this before. 'They feel as if they are on fire.'

'That's a good sign,' Melissa said as she looked down towards Charli's toes. 'It means the circulation is working. Blood is reaching your feet and toes as you warm up. Colour is returning to your toes. We should be able to save them. I can give you something for the pain.'

Charli nodded and concentrated on attempting to breathe through the pain, while Melissa ordered intravenous pain relief.

'Has that pain relief worked?' the doctor asked as she finished suturing the wound in Charli's palm.

Charli's feet felt like two enormous soccer balls at the ends of her legs but the burning sensation had decreased slightly. Her feet still felt hot but it was better. Almost bearable. She nodded.

'Do you need anything else,' Melissa asked, 'before we get ready to transfer you?'

She was exhausted, overwrought, hungry and filthy. She wanted a hot bath and some clean clothes, something to eat and for people to stop poking her and sticking needles into her. But what she got was a drip in her arm, some antiseptic wipes and a hospital gown.

She wanted to sleep.

She wanted to wake up somewhere familiar and safe.

She wanted Patrick.

Charli wanted to see his face again in case it really was the last time.

But her brain had shut down, whether from exhaustion or stress or trauma she wasn't sure, but whatever the reason she found she could no longer string a coherent sentence together. She didn't know how to ask for what she wanted. How to ask for Patrick.

But he was there anyway. He appeared beside her as if he knew what she needed almost before she did. His red uniform and dark hair stood out in stark contrast to the white surroundings. Seeing him immediately calmed her racing heart.

He came to stand on her left side and she instinctively reached out for him, unsure just when she had become so dependent on him but certain that he would take her hand. He would offer comfort.

'Hey.' He smiled and she relaxed. 'I hear you're in pretty good shape.'

He didn't tell her she looked better or brighter but he did take her hand. She could only imagine what she looked like. Bloodied, bruised and filthy. She would look like someone who had been buried alive for forty hours. She knew her blonde hair was matted and dirty. She could feel that her left eye, just under the cut on her forehead, was partially closed from swelling and she imagined it was turning purple. She suspected she looked like the victim of a mugging or a car accident.

'Melissa tells me you're stable enough to be transferred to Melbourne.'

'Melbourne?' She knew that but her brain was taking a long time to catch up to what she was hearing and even longer to process information. She was sure she wasn't concussed. She just needed to eat and sleep, then everything would be back to normal.

'The helicopter is on its way to take you to the Princess Elizabeth Hospital.'

'By myself?' She looked at Pat, waiting for his answer, knowing it wasn't going to be the one she wanted to hear.

Pat could see a cascade of emotions in her blue eyes. Pleading, longing, desperation, fear, worry and loneliness. He knew she was asking him to accompany her.

She was waiting for his answer but he couldn't do it. He was already breaking protocol by being at the medical centre. His shift should have ended the minute Charli had been extracted from the rubble. He'd worked overtime and he was supposed to be resting. He could argue that he was off duty, though he couldn't pretend he was resting. But he wasn't going to abandon Charli now. He'd stay with her until she was on the helicopter. Stay with her for as long as possible. He wasn't ready to say goodbye.

He saw Melissa glance at his hand, where Charli's fingers had entwined with his. Could Melissa tell that Pat was holding on just as firmly? Could she tell he didn't want to let her go?

'I'll give you a moment,' Melissa said as she turned and left the room. Leaving them truly alone for the first time.

He knew Charli had formed a bond with him while she'd been trapped. He knew. He felt it too. But if he was asked to explain it, he wouldn't be able to. It had to be fate that had put him in her path, or her in his. He didn't really know. All he knew was that she was important to him.

But he couldn't leave the mountain. He wasn't dismissed from duty. He would have to take his break and then get back to work. He couldn't go to Melbourne. He still had a job to do here. He didn't want her to go without him, he didn't want to say goodbye, but he didn't have a choice.

'I can't leave the mountain,' he told her. 'We still have work to do. Amy will go with you.'

She nodded. Her eyes were teary but the tears did not spill over. The moisture turned them a more startling shade of blue. He shouldn't be noticing things like that but he couldn't help it.

'Will I see you again?' she asked.

He nodded. 'I'll come and see you as soon as I can,' he said, and he knew it was a promise he would do everything he could to keep.

Charli had spent two days in the Princess Elizabeth Hospital in Melbourne staring at the walls. Two days with mostly only her thoughts for company. And her thoughts were far from pleasant. She was clean and she'd eaten and she was starting to feel more human, although she still longed for a shower. The nurses had tried but the pain in her feet was so intense she hadn't been able to stand or walk. They had tried to transfer her to a shower chair but even lowering her feet was too painful. She'd had to make do with a bed bath.

The nurses had put the television on yesterday but it had seemed to be showing a constant tale of the disaster in Wombat Gully and Charli had switched it off and had kept it turned it off. She couldn't bear to watch or listen to any more of the stories being told. The reporters had no idea what it had been like. They had no idea how it had felt to be buried alive, how scared she'd been, how cold, how lonely.

But she hadn't expected to still feel lonely. She wasn't good at being by herself.

She knew her fear of being alone stemmed from losing her mother at a young age, and usually she felt better if Amy was nearby. Amy was her someone, but even though her sister had made the trip to Melbourne and was keeping her company, it wasn't enough to keep the doldrums at bay. She missed Pat.

She knew he wasn't the answer, he couldn't fix her fears or dispel her depression, but she still hoped he'd come to see her as he'd promised.

He had said she would see him again but she had no idea if or when. Maybe he hadn't meant it.

She lay on her back with the sheets tented over her swollen and painful feet. She had her head turned to the wall, ignoring the door, feeling sorry for herself.

'Hey.'

She turned at the sound of a voice. *His* voice. She recognised it instantly. 'Pat! What are you doing here?'

'I told you I would come as soon as I could.'

She'd hoped to see him but as the days had passed she'd convinced herself that he hadn't meant it. He had a family to go home to. Why would he come to see her? But she wasn't going to pretend she wasn't pleased to see him. She couldn't believe he was here. And she couldn't stop the smile that was spreading across her face. She wondered briefly if she should be so transparent but she figured she might as well let him know she appreciated his visit.

He held two takeaway cups in his hand. 'I brought you the hot chocolate I promised,' he said, as he passed her a cup.

'I can't believe you remembered. Thank you.'

'There's one for Amy too. Isn't she here?'

'She's gone to the airport to pick up our father.'

Her tone was less than enthusiastic and Pat responded to it. 'Aren't you looking forward to seeing him?'

'Not particularly. I can't believe she rang him.'

Pat was frowning. 'Why wouldn't she?'

'I know you're close to your brother and I assume to your parents too, but it's not like that for me and Amy. We're not at the top of his list of priorities. I'm surprised he's even coming.'

'But you're his daughters. Surely if you need him, he's there for you?'

'We don't need him. We haven't needed him in a long time. We've learnt to manage on our own.'

'What do you mean by that?'

'Our mother died when I was seven. Dad was never the same after that. I know he loved us, we had been the centre of their world, but after Mum died it was almost as though he couldn't bear to have us around. We assumed we reminded him of everything he'd lost. When Dad married Victoria we were sent off to boarding school. I was ten.'

'Ten! That's a bit young, isn't it?'

'It is, but it's not unusual in the UK, especially for wealthier families. Lots of children go to boarding school but it wasn't something that was on the agenda for us, at least it wasn't while our mother was alive. But Victoria isn't the maternal type. She is very career focussed and I don't think she ever wanted to be responsible for raising another woman's children and we were sent away. Our father had other priorities, his work and Victoria. We haven't spent much time with him for years.'

Charli's bedside phone rang, interrupting their discussion. She breathed a sigh of relief. 'Would you mind answering that?' she asked. 'I don't want to speak to anyone.'

She could tell from his side of the conversation who it was and she watched as Pat scribbled a note on a piece of paper.

'That was another news station wanting to interview me, wasn't it?' she said as he hung up the phone.

Pat nodded. 'Have you had lots?'

'Quite a few. I've told the nurses I don't want to speak to reporters. I don't have the energy and I can't imagine why they'd be interested in my story. I'm not even Australian. Surely they can find someone else to interview? I figured one of the other survivors might be happy to do it.'

'Charli…' Pat ran his fingers through his hair, making it spike up. He looked exhausted and she wondered how much sleep he'd had in the past few days. 'Haven't you been watching the news?'

'No. It was all about the landslide. I didn't

want to relive it so I've kept the television off. Why?' she asked.

Pat rubbed his jaw. 'There weren't any other survivors,' he told her. 'You're the only one.'

'What?' She frowned, thinking she must have misheard him. 'I can't be. There were fifteen other people missing. You've found them all?'

He nodded.

'They're all dead?'

He nodded again.

'Oh, my God, those poor people.' Charli's eyes filled with tears but before they had a chance to spill over Pat was sitting beside her on the bed and had wrapped his arm around her. She let her tears flow as Pat rubbed her back. The pressure of his hand was firm but gentle. She didn't know how but, once again, he had the knack, either through his words or a smile or a touch of his hand, of being able to soothe her. She wondered when she would run out of tears; she had cried more in the past few weeks than she had in the past twenty years.

Burying her face in his shoulder, she let him comfort her until she thought she could speak without crying. She lifted her head and rubbed the tears from her face. 'I'm sorry.'

'It's okay.' He brushed a tear from her cheek with his thumb. 'You've had a traumatic experience. It's a normal reaction.'

But Charli was mortified. She couldn't believe she'd been whinging about her father when fifteen other people were dead. She was safe. Pat and his colleagues had risked their lives for her and she was being self-absorbed. It wasn't all about her. In fact, it wasn't about her at all. 'How are you and your team?' she asked. 'It must have been awful. Finding no one.'

'We found you,' he replied simply, as if that was enough. Maybe, under the circumstances, it was.

She smiled. 'Yes, you did.'

'What time are you expecting Amy?'

'Soon, I think. Why?'

'I have to go. I don't want to leave you alone if you're feeling fragile but I haven't seen my daughter yet.'

'You came here instead?'

He nodded.

'Why?'

'I wanted to see you and if I went home

first I wasn't sure that I'd get away again, but if I don't go soon she'll be in bed and it will be another day that I haven't kissed her good-night. After days like we've just had I really need to do that. For me, more than for her.'

He stood up and Charli noticed he was still in his uniform. She hadn't seen him in anything else so it hadn't seemed significant until now. She couldn't believe he'd come to see her first, before anything else. It was no wonder he looked exhausted. She needed to let him leave. 'You should go,' she said. 'I'm fine.'

As much as she didn't want him to leave, she knew she couldn't ask him to stay. She was resilient. She would be fine. His daughter needed him more.

'I'll come back tomorrow,' he told her. 'Is there anything you need me to bring you?'

She and Amy had lost everything in the landslide. Granted it hadn't been their entire possessions but all they had left was Amy's phone and wallet. All of Charli's belongings were gone.

'I need to do something about replacing my stuff,' she said. 'I lost my phone and pass-port. I can ring my insurance company but the policy number and all the details were in my phone. Amy will get me a phone but I need access to email.' Keeping busy, making a list of what she needed to do and ticking things off as she went would keep her busy for now.

'I'll bring in a laptop you can borrow. Would that help?'

She nodded. 'Thank you, that would be great.'

'Okay, I'll see you tomorrow.'

He leant over and kissed her on the forehead and Charli's heart flipped in her chest. She caught her breath and hoped she wasn't turning bright red from embarrassment. He had done it so casually she wondered if he'd even noticed, but she certainly had.

She waited until he left the room and then pressed her fingers to the spot where his lips had rested. She'd gone from feeling sad and lonely to elated and hopeful.

She lay back on the bed with a smile on her face as she counted her blessings. She was alive and so was Amy. Her injuries were minor. Pat had come to see her and he would come back again. And he'd kissed her.

Maybe something good would come out of the tragedy. Maybe there was something to look forward to in the days ahead.

CHAPTER SEVEN

HE'D KISSED HER without thinking yesterday. Automatically. But it had felt entirely natural and she hadn't seemed to mind. But he hadn't waited around to find out. He was telling himself it had been a spur-of-the-moment thing but, in all honesty, he'd been wanting to kiss her since he'd first met her, since the night she'd literally fallen into his arms at the bar and he'd walked her home.

The feeling had only intensified as he'd talked to her through the hours that she'd been trapped and then when he'd joined her in her tomb-like space. He wanted to taste her, to hold her in his arms for a reason other than providing comfort or safety. A kiss on the forehead wasn't enough. All it had done was serve to whet his desire even more.

Wanting to take something further with a woman was a new experience for him.

He'd been on a couple of dates in the past two years but neither of them had gone well. Friends had set him up and he'd gone along with their plans out of politeness, but he hadn't wanted to have a second date with either of the women and he'd discouraged any further suggestions from well-meaning friends and colleagues. But things were different with Charli. His interest was definitely piqued. He'd only felt this sense of excitement and anticipation once before. When he'd first met his wife.

Was he being disloyal to Margie? To her memory? To the life they'd shared?

He waited for the sense of betrayal to hit him but there was nothing. No guilt, no recriminations. The life he'd had with Margie was over. He had Ella but that relationship, while precious, wasn't enough to sustain him. He needed more. He knew he still wasn't ready for, or looking for, anything serious or permanent but needed adult company, a physical relationship, physical intimacy, and Charli was the first woman he'd met that he could imagine taking that step with. That he wanted to take that step with.

If he hadn't come straight from Wombat

Gully to the hospital yesterday he would have stayed longer with her. If he hadn't needed a shower and something to eat, if he hadn't needed to see his daughter. But he'd had to spend time with Ella and it was now late in the afternoon, almost tea time in the hospital, less than two hours until he started a night shift, and he couldn't wait to get back to see Charli again.

He was approaching Charli's room when a tall man with greying hair, an upright posture and a confident walk came through her door and headed for the nurses' station. His bearing was controlled and purposeful but Pat recognised sorrow in his eyes.

It had to be Charli's father. He looked like he was working hard to hold it together.

Pat watched him walk away before he continued on into Charli's room.

He pushed open the door and found her lying in bed and she looked upset too. Immediately he wanted to comfort her, to take her in his arms and kiss her better, but he wasn't sure that he had that right. Yesterday's actions had been spontaneous but he couldn't presume that she would welcome any further violation of her personal space.

But something about her brought out all his protective instincts. She had an air of fragility about her but she wasn't fragile, she'd shown that throughout her ordeal, but she seemed delicate. Was it her appearance? Her enormous blue eyes, her porcelain skin or the circumstances of her rescue that bound him to her? He didn't know but she'd certainly got under his defences. He thought about her constantly but had no idea what could come of this attraction.

He looked over his shoulder, making sure the doorway was clear. 'That man who just left your room? Was that your father?' he asked. She nodded and he looked around the room. 'Did he come alone?'

'What do you mean?'

The room was empty save for him and Charli. 'Your stepmother. She's not here?'

'No. Apparently her doctor advised her not to fly, although I'm not sure she would have come anyway.'

He frowned. 'Why? What's the matter with her?'

'She's eight months pregnant. Eight months!' Charli's eyebrows arched wildly. 'Can you believe it?' She didn't wait for his response, which was just as well as he really had no opinion to offer. 'She's pregnant and this is the first I've heard of it.'

'Why are you so upset?'

Charli gave a heavy, exasperated sigh. 'I don't understand my father at all. He married someone almost half his age and sent Amy and me to boarding school. He couldn't wait to get rid of us and now he's starting all over again. Victoria didn't want children and now suddenly she's pregnant at the age of thirty-nine. It's crazy.'

'Maybe this is a good thing.'

She looked at him like he'd gone mad. She wasn't upset, he realised. She was angry. 'How can this be a good thing?'

He knew she was struggling emotionally after the landslide. It wasn't an unusual response after a traumatic experience, but maybe this would give her something to look forward to. A baby was the perfect distraction. He knew that from his own experience. 'A new life brings hope. This baby will be a half-sibling. This baby will be family.'

'One who is twenty-six years younger than me!' she countered. 'That's not a sibling. That poor child, having to be a part of our family, having Victoria and my father as parents. It'll probably be shunted off to boarding school too at the earliest opportunity, unwanted and unloved.'

'Are you sure you're not being a bit harsh?'

'No.' She shook her head. 'You don't know my father.'

Pat thought about the man he'd seen leaving Charli's room just minutes ago and the sadness he'd seen in his eyes. 'Don't you think he might love you the best way he knows how? He's flown halfway across the world to see you.'

'And he can't wait to get home again. He's already told me he doesn't want to leave Victoria alone for too long.'

'Things are rarely that black and white.'

'Oh, I think they are. I have spent years trying to figure out why I don't have a relationship with my father but I've got nowhere. I have loved my medical training and I can't wait to start the next stage towards becoming a GP, but one of the reasons I chose medicine was because I thought it might make my father proud of me. I thought it might make him take an interest in me but nothing changed.

'I know it was easy for Amy and me to

blame our stepmother's influence but even if it was her decision to send us away, I can't really believe that my father, an intelligent, accomplished man, would have followed her lead if he didn't agree with her. At the end of the day he paid for our education but didn't put much time or effort into maintaining or even establishing a relationship with either of us. Even now, all he can think about is getting back home. He's not thinking about me or Amy, it's all about him and Victoria.'

'But he's here *now*. Doesn't that count for something?'

Charli was shaking her head. 'He's never around when I need him and so I've learnt not to need him, and I *definitely* don't need him now.'

Pat knew he wouldn't win any arguments with Charli about her family. He didn't know her father—he could have been imagining what he'd seen in his expression, in his eyes. He could have been projecting what his feelings as a father would be if Ella was lying in hospital. He knew he would be heartbroken, but he had to take Charli's word for her father's actions and feelings. At least for now.

He nodded and decided to change the subject. He opened the bag he'd brought with him, pulling out various bits of electronic equipment. 'I brought you my laptop. If I set you up a profile and a password, can you access your emails remotely?'

He saw her take a deep breath to regain her composure before saying, 'Yes, thank you.'

'I'm working night shift but I'll leave it with you.'

He flipped the laptop open and fired it up. His screensaver appeared. He was so used to it that he didn't give it a second thought until Charli said, 'Is that your family?'

The photo was one of him with Margie and Ella. He had taken a photo of the three of them in bed on Christmas morning. It had been their first Christmas as a family. Ella had only been eight months old, too young to understand Christmas, but he and Margie had been very excited about the next stage of their life together as a family, celebrating all these milestones with their daughter and anticipating the future. They'd been happy. Really happy.

Of course, they hadn't known then it would be their only Christmas as a family.

'Is that your wife?' He could hear the

puzzlement in Charli's voice. 'Aren't you divorced?' The puzzlement was now an accusation.

'No, I'm not divorced.'

'You said you and your daughter lived in Melbourne. You told me you weren't married. You invited me for brunch!'

'I'm not married or divorced,' he explained. 'I'm a widower.'

'Oh, Pat, I'm sorry. I just assumed. You never said…'

Her tone was contrite and perhaps a little guilty.

'What should I have said?'

'I don't know,' she said with a shake of her head. 'When I asked if you were married, why didn't you tell me then?'

'I didn't want to talk about someone who had died. Not in those circumstances.'

'I'm sorry, I didn't know. I didn't mean to bring it up.'

'It's okay. I don't mind talking about her. I need to keep her memory alive for Ella and I'm getting used to being alone.'

'How long ago did she die?'

'Two years.'

'So your daughter would have been very young.'

Pat nodded.

'That must have been an awful time for you. How are you doing now?'

'I'm good. We're good, Ella and I.'

'Do you want to tell me about her?'

'About who?'

'Your wife.'

'Why?'

She shrugged. 'I feel like you know everything about me but I know almost nothing about you.'

What did she want to hear? What did she want him to say? He had never had a problem talking about Margie, it had been a way of keeping her memory alive, but he'd always talked to people who had known her. Talking to Charli would be different. But she was right, he knew far more about her and he didn't want Margie to come between them and whatever this connection was. Wherever this was going. And he was definite that he wanted this to go somewhere. He'd known his past and his future would collide at some point and it looked like today was the day. He took a deep breath and said, 'What do you want to know?'

'How long were you married?'

'Three years.'

'That's not long.'

'No, it wasn't nearly long enough.'

'Where did you meet?'

'In the UK.'

'She was English?'

'No. Her grandfather was but Margie was Australian. She was a nurse, from Melbourne. I was on a working visa as a paramedic and she was an ED nurse in one of the large hospitals. We travelled half way around the world to fall in love with someone from home. We used to laugh about that.'

'What happened to her? Was she sick?'

'No. She was perfectly healthy. She was in an accident.' He sighed. Her death had been so senseless, so unnecessary and such a shock, which had made it hard to comprehend and even harder to accept. 'Ella had just turned one and Margie had not long returned to work. She was on a late. Her shifts had to work around my roster but that was okay— we were used to the shift work and it meant someone was always there for Ella. She was in her car, stopped at traffic lights. The lights turned green but as she went through the intersection some kids in a stolen car ran the red light and crashed into her. She died at the scene.'

'Oh, Pat. That's so sudden. It must have been such a shock.'

He nodded. 'Margie always used to worry about my job and the associated risks. We always thought there was more of a chance of something happening to me because of the job I did, but it turned out it wasn't my job we needed to concern ourselves about. It turned out that no one is safe. I should have known that better than anyone. Margie was in the wrong place at the wrong time. I struggled for a long time with guilt. I save lives for a living but I couldn't save Margie.'

'But you're doing okay now?'

'Yes.'

'How long did that take?'

'A long time,' he admitted. 'Gradually I have made memories that don't involve her, which is painful at times, but slowly those new memories dull the loss and it becomes easier to cope with. Now there are things I can think about that don't automatically make me think about her too. I had to go on because of Ella but I've only recently got to a place where I'm looking forward to the future, where I can imagine a different future, one without Margie in it.'

'Have you dated since Margie died?'

'Not seriously.'

'Why not?'

'Lots of reasons.' Initially he'd felt he was betraying Margie's memory and as the dates had been casual he'd preferred to sacrifice the date rather than his late wife's memory. That had changed with meeting Charli but he wasn't sure how to phrase that without sounding like he was trying out a line. 'I haven't met anyone I really wanted to date or who I was prepared to introduce to Ella. She's already lost one mother, I need to think carefully about how my actions will impact on her if things don't work out. Ella and I are okay as a unit of two.'

'I bet she was a good mother.'

'She was a fabulous mother. We were so excited when we found out she was pregnant. It's tough being a single parent but having Ella was the thing that really pulled me through after Margie died. I had to keep going, for her.'

'How do you manage? It can't be easy, especially not with shift work.'

'I have a *lot* of help. My parents and my in-laws live close by and Ella also goes to child care when I work. Speaking of which, I really have to get to work.' He hoped what he'd told her would be enough to satisfy her for now. He set up a password for her on his laptop and headed off, resisting the urge to kiss her again.

'You did well. How're you feeling?' Harriet said as she accompanied Charli back to her bed after her physiotherapy session.

Charli's feet were still heavily bandaged but Harriet had given her a pair of shoes made from pieces of foam and rubber, which cushioned her feet, and she was able now to stand with a walking frame and get herself to the bathroom. Her gait was still slow and she couldn't be upright for too long as her feet remained painful, but it was a nice change to be able to stand, even briefly.

'You might be able to get out of here in another couple of days, once I can get you on

crutches,' the physio said. 'I'll bring you a
pair tomorrow and you can try walking with
them. Once you can manage stairs, you'll be
able to be discharged.'

'When do you think I'll be able to fly?'

'Not for a little while yet. Your feet are still
too swollen, and the risk of clots is too high.
Why do you ask?'

'I haven't got anywhere to go once I'm discharged. I need to think about flying home.'

'Where is Amy staying?'

'She has to go back to Wombat Gully tomorrow. It's the start of the school holidays
and they need her for ski school.' Charli
shrugged. 'I guess I'll have to stay with my
father in the hotel.' That wouldn't be ideal
as she and her father didn't have the easiest
of relationships, but she didn't have another
choice.

'I thought you said he wanted to go home
soon?' Harriet queried, raising another ob-
stacle. 'What if he leaves before you're ready
to fly? Why don't you stay with your cute
paramedic?'

'Patrick? He's not *my* paramedic.'

'What do you mean?' Harriet said. 'I thought
you were an item. Are you just friends?'

Charli didn't know how to describe their relationship. She had spent quite a bit of time with Harriet over the past few days. The nurses bustled in and out, too busy to talk, but the physiotherapist had become something of a confidante to her, though they hadn't discussed Pat. 'I'm not sure what we are. I think he feels a sense of duty to me. He was the one who pulled me from the building.'

'I don't think he's here out of duty,' Harriet said. 'Have you seen the way he looks at you? I swear he wants to sweep you off your feet and take you away from here. He's your knight in shining armour. If he had a horse I could just imagine him riding in here on his noble steed.' She sighed. 'I've always wanted one of them.'

'A noble steed?' Charli smiled.

'A hero!'

'You've been watching too many movies.'

'No,' she said with a laugh. 'Reading too many books probably.'

Charli shook her head. 'I couldn't impose on Patrick like that.' She'd had the same fantasy of Pat as her real-life hero—he had rescued her after all—but that didn't mean he was about to sweep her off her feet and run away with her, and she didn't feel she could ask him to. She had no idea if they had that sort of relationship and listening to how he'd spoken about his late wife and daughter, Charli wasn't sure that he saw any sort of romantic relationship in his immediate future. She didn't want to put him in a difficult position, she was pretty sure that if she was brave enough to ask, the answer would be no. 'I'll discuss it with my father. He's meeting Amy and me here to take us to lunch.'

Just the mention of lunch with her father was enough to make her feel nervous. He'd suggested lunch and they were only going to the street-level coffee shop at the front of the hospital, but Charli suspected there was something her father wanted to discuss. She couldn't imagine him arranging lunch with his daughters for no reason.

'Let's get you changed.' Harriet grabbed a suit bag that she had hung behind the door when she'd arrived for the physio session. She'd offered to lend Charli a dress for lunch as the two of them were a similar size and Charli had absolutely nothing to wear. She could hardly go to the coffee shop in a hospital gown. She'd ordered some clothes online, using Pat's laptop and Amy's credit card, but, as yet, nothing had been delivered. It had been a surreal experience to be lying in a hospital bed, doing online shopping.

Harriet unzipped the bag and pulled out some new underwear, a navy wrap dress in a stretchy cotton and a white shirt and simple black jeans. She held them up. 'Will one of these do?'

'The dress,' Charli said. She would need to wear the shoes that Harriet had made for her and thought they might look less ridiculous with the dress, although anything was going to be better than the hospital gowns she had spent the past few days wearing. 'Thank you so much, Harriet.'

'Do you need a hand to get changed or can you manage?'

'I'll be fine.'

'All right, I'll guard the door for you and then fetch a wheelchair to take you down to the coffee shop.'

As the door closed behind Harriet, Charli stripped off the hospital gown and left it on the end of the bed. She tossed the uncomfortable and unflattering disposable undies into the bin and replaced them with the pair

Harriet had given her. She wrapped the dress around herself, pulling the ties tight. It was a little loose on her—she'd lost weight over the past week—but it would do. She brushed her hair and tied it back into a ponytail. She couldn't do anything about her make-up, but it wasn't an occasion that warranted any.

There was a knock on her door. 'I'm decent,' she called.

'That's the worst news I've heard all morning. Should I come back when you're indecent?'

She had assumed it was Harriet knocking but the door had opened to reveal Pat.

He was grinning at her and her heart flipped in her chest as Harriet's words rang in her ears. Did he have feelings for her?

The idea thrilled her and terrified her at the same time but she couldn't deny she was attracted to him. Who could blame her? He was gorgeous. He wore a pair of bone-coloured cotton trousers and a grey shirt that highlighted his olive complexion and hugged his chest. It was the first time she'd seen him out of uniform and, incredibly, he looked even more amazing.

She smiled, unable to pretend she wasn't excited to see him.

'You look good. Are you going somewhere?' he asked as Harriet appeared with a wheelchair and Charli tried to ignore the knowing smirk on the physio's face.

'Amy and I are having lunch with my father.'

He looked a little crestfallen and she wondered if he'd had other plans. For the first time he looked as if he wasn't going to work or rushing off to pick up Ella. Not that she minded, she knew his daughter came first and she couldn't begrudge that, not when it was exactly how she wished her own father had prioritised things. Ella was lucky to have Pat for a father, she thought, not for the first time.

'Let me help you into this chair,' he said as he slid his hands under her thighs and scooped her off the bed. Her arms automatically wound around his neck as he held her close. She breathed in, inhaling the scent of freshly washed skin and soap.

'You do know the hospital has a no-lift policy,' Harriet told him as he set Charli down in the wheelchair and she reluctantly unwound her arms from his neck.

'Good thing I'm not employed by the hospital then, isn't it?' Pat laughed as he spun the chair around to face the door.

Charli was still smiling when her father walked into the room.

'Charlotte! I thought I was meeting you here?' He looked from Charli to Pat.

'Mr Lawson.' Patrick spoke before Charli had a chance to and extended his hand. 'I'm Patrick Reeves.'

'Reeves?' her father said. 'I've heard your name before. You rescued Charlotte from the building.'

'I did.'

'Thank you.' He reached for Pat's hand and shook it. 'Please, call me Jack. You're a paramedic, I believe?'

Charli sat in semi-uncomfortable silence and listened to the easy conversation between her father and Pat while they discussed his job as he wheeled her out into the corridor towards the lift. Charli couldn't remember ever having an easy conversation with her father about anything.

'Would you like to join us for lunch?' Her father extended an invitation to Pat.

'Thank you, but I can't. Maybe another time.'

Charli wished he would. Maybe then she wouldn't have to endure a stilted conversation or listen to whatever bad news she was certain her father was going to deliver.

The lift arrived and Pat let her father take over, leaving Charli to wonder what the purpose of Pat's visit had been.

Pat was back at the hospital as early as possible the following day. He wanted to check on Charli. He'd sensed she'd been nervous about lunch with her father and he wanted to see her just to make sure she was okay.

He pushed open her hospital door and was confronted by an empty room. There was a travel bag on the bed, clothes folded and set in a pile beside it.

Amy came out of the bathroom, carrying a small cosmetics bag.

'What's going on?' Pat asked just as the door opened behind him. Harriet was holding it as Charli stepped through with the aid of crutches. Pat was surprised. When he'd seen her yesterday, she'd still been using a wheelchair.

'She's made good progress,' the physiotherapist commented when she saw Pat's expression.

'The doctors are ready to discharge me,' Charli added.

'You can fly?'

'Not yet. Walking with crutches is enough. Flying is not one of my superpowers.' She smiled and Pat was relieved. Maybe yesterday's lunch had gone well.

But his relief was short-lived. If she was recovering physically and emotionally and was ready for discharge, that meant she would be leaving. Leaving the hospital and one step closer to leaving Melbourne. One step closer to being out of his life. 'Is your father coming to get you?'

She shook her head. 'No. He's gone.'

'Gone where?'

'Back to England.'

Pat frowned. 'Without you?' He had assumed that Jack would stay until Charli was ready to fly. He'd assumed her father would travel with her.

'That was what lunch was all about.' Charli glanced at Amy. 'He was telling us he's leaving.'

'Why?' Pat was totally confused.

'My stepmother is having complications with the pregnancy. As usual, she trumps me. Us. Dad is concerned because, apparently, Victoria is having twins, which was a bit of information he neglected to pass on initially.'

He could hear the effort she made to keep her tone light but he knew she would be hurting. She'd said enough for him to know that her father's reserve bothered her, that she felt he had abandoned her on more than one occasion. But he wondered if her father's departure was as straightforward as Charli believed. All relationships were complicated and he wondered if she was expecting things to be black and white when in reality they were usually shades of grey. He'd seen Jack's expression when he'd visited Charli and Pat's opinion was that Jack was a man who felt things but perhaps had learned to keep his emotions hidden.

But Pat knew it wasn't his place to interfere. He didn't know their history. He'd only heard one side of the story. And that didn't change the fact that Jack had left, had returned to England, once again choosing his wife over his daughter, or, as he expected Charli would see it, abandoning her yet again.

He looked at the small pile of her possessions on the bed, reflecting the little she had left in her world. 'Where are you going to go?' He turned to Amy. 'Is she coming to stay with you?'

'No, I have to head back to Wombat Gully tonight.'

He looked back to Charli, who shrugged her shoulders. 'I guess I'll book a hotel room.'

'I don't think you're quite ready to be on your own yet, Charli,' Harriet said. 'I know you're mobile but you *are* still on crutches.'

Pat looked at the physio. 'Should she be being discharged then?'

'She meets the criteria and I think getting out of here would be good. The media are still ringing constantly, wanting an interview, so leaving might avoid that stress.'

He looked at Charli, making a snap decision. 'You can stay with me.'

'I couldn't do that.'

'Why not?'

'That sounds like a perfect solution,' Harriet interrupted. 'I'll let the two of you sort out the details and I'll let the nurses know to start your discharge paperwork.' She spun on her heel and left the room.

Charli was looking at him warily.

'What are your objections?' he asked her.

'What would you tell your daughter?' she queried as she sat on the edge of her bed.

'Don't worry about Ella,' he replied as he took the crutches from her and leant them against the wall. 'My in-laws have taken her interstate to visit her cousins. She won't be home. But I wasn't planning on taking you to my house. I have somewhere better in mind. My family has a house in the country. It's the perfect place for some R and R. There's no cell phone reception. It will just be the two of us.'

'I've seen that movie, *Wolf Creek*...'

'I promise I have honourable intentions.' While he may have entertained some less-than-honourable thoughts, his intentions were genuine. He wanted to help. They were friends first, and if she wanted to keep it that way he would respect her wishes. He wanted her to feel safe with him.

'Amy will know where you are. I have four days off. Let me help. What do you think?'

He stepped closer, making a pretence of adjusting the pillows on her bed. Charli wriggled backwards and he scooped her legs up, lifting them for her. She was wearing a pair of gym shorts and her legs were virtually bare. His forearm was under her thighs, skin against bare skin. He was deliberately testing the water, testing her reaction. He saw her pupils dilate. He knew she felt the same connection. Whenever he held her in his arms he never wanted to let her go. She was casting a spell and he was falling under it, fast. It was good for his ego to know he was having a similar effect on her too.

'Would you like to run away with me?'

She smiled and his heart flipped. He knew she was going to say yes.

'I think that sounds wonderful.'

'Pat?' Amy's voice surprised him. He'd forgotten she was also in the room. 'Could you give us a minute?'

Amy waited until Pat left the room but Charli could tell from her sister's expression that she was about to get the third degree.

'Do you think this is a good idea?' Amy asked.

'What?'

'Going to stay with Pat.'

'I don't see the problem?'

'You don't think this is another knee-jerk reaction?'

'A knee-jerk reaction? To what?'

Amy sighed. 'To everything that has happened. To you being trapped. To Hugo's behaviour. To Dad leaving so quickly. I worry that every time Dad disappoints you, you try to find someone who will stay by your side, but you have to admit your choices haven't always been great. Wouldn't you be better off coming with me? I'm going to stay with Daniel, I'm sure he wouldn't mind if you stayed too.'

'I think he might,' Charli retorted, 'but anyway I can't go back to Wombat Gully. Not yet. Maybe not ever. I don't think I could bear it.'

'I just don't want to see you get hurt again. I know you're attracted to Pat but I don't want you to think he is the answer.'

'To what?'

'To giving you a safe haven.'

'That's not what this is,' she replied. 'It's fine, it's not for ever. I'm not *expecting* it to be for ever. I'm supposed to be home to start my GP training in a few weeks.'

'Are you sure? You don't think you're putting yourself in a vulnerable position?'

'What does that mean?'

Amy raised her hands in protest when she saw Charli's expression. 'Don't get me wrong,' she clarified. 'I really like him, but he has plenty of baggage and so do you. He's a single dad, he's got lots of other commitments and responsibilities. You're still recovering from your ordeal, physically and emotionally. Do you think staying with him is wise? Would you stay with him if you *weren't* attracted to him?'

She knew she wouldn't but if she lied she also knew that Amy would see straight through her. 'I'd probably ask Harriet if there were any other options,' she admitted.

'Are you strong enough to handle things if they go wrong again? I'm not saying they will, but you need to at least consider that.'

Charli hesitated. Amy had a point. She *did* tend to romanticise things—people and situations—but she had spent a lot of time thinking about her life while she'd been trapped. About her mother and father. About her stepmother. About Hugo.

After her mother had died and their father

had remarried, she had felt as though all she'd had left in the world was Amy. It had been the two of them alone. All she'd wanted was to feel loved and cared for, to feel important to someone, and she had spent most of her life looking for that person.

She knew now that she'd thrown herself into her relationship with Hugo without stopping to examine if he was right for her. She'd been so desperate to belong to someone that it hadn't mattered whether or not he was perfect for her—all that had mattered was that he showed her interest and attention. But their relationship hadn't been enough for him. *She* hadn't been enough for him. She was never enough for anyone.

She couldn't believe she'd been so naïve as to think Hugo had been the one for her. She couldn't believe that it had taken this crazy situation to give her some perspective on her life and on her own behaviour. Because she couldn't lay all the blame at Hugo's feet. She had to take some responsibility or risk making the same mistakes over and over again. She had made a promise to herself while she'd been trapped that when she got out she would focus on her career. Hopefully that would be something she could control, and she would take a break from trying to find the perfect relationship.

'I'm not looking for someone to run off into the sunset with,' she said. 'This will just be for a few days. As soon as I can fly I'll be going home.'

She wasn't planning on staying indefinitely. This time *she* would be the one leaving, on her terms. She couldn't deny she was attracted to Patrick but she was convinced she could handle it.

Charli slept most of the way while Pat drove, and only woke up when he bumped over a cattle grate as he turned off the bitumen and onto a rough, potholed dirt road. Sheep grazed in the paddocks on either side of the road and ahead of her a lake glistened in the afternoon light.

The view was breath-taking. Rolling green hills, plump white sheep, stately eucalyptus trees and the dark blue of the lake all nestled under a clear blue winter sky. '*This* is where you grew up?'

This wasn't what she'd expected when Pat had asked her to run away with him. This idyllic, secluded spot. Her heart raced with a mixture of nervousness and anticipation.

She had been on an emotional roller-coaster ever since the disaster, and her father's most recent abandonment to support his wife had reopened past wounds. She was exhausted, tired of thinking about her father, tired of being in pain, tired of constantly refusing interview requests. Even while she'd been forced to admit that perhaps Amy had a point, she hadn't been able to refuse Pat's offer of a place to stay.

Maybe it was a place to run and hide. Maybe running away was becoming a thing for her. She'd chosen a medical school far from home so she'd have to live in. She'd chosen to run to Amy rather than face a showdown with Hugo. Each time someone let her down, that was her response. But she enjoyed Pat's company, she enjoyed the way he made her feel, and she hadn't wanted to refuse his invitation. Maybe she was running away again but she'd made her decision. She was in Pat's car and about to spend a few days alone with him.

She wondered what the next few days would bring. Would it give them the time and space she wanted, needed, to explore the possibilities between them?

She swallowed nervously and took a deep breath as Pat nodded and turned in behind a weatherboard house that sat on a rise overlooking the lake. It was painted cream with a grey tin roof and wide steps led up to verandas which wrapped around three sides. Vines crawled up the veranda posts and a post-and-rail fence protected the garden beds from the grazing sheep.

'Are those your sheep?'

Pat shook his head. 'My parents leased the land to one of the neighbours when they moved to Melbourne. The sheep are his.'

He switched the engine off and Charli opened her door. Pat handed her the crutches as she swung her legs out of the car.

He had their bags in his hands. 'I'll come back for you and help you with the stairs,' he said. 'Just let me open up.'

'I can manage. Harriet wouldn't let me be discharged unless I could negotiate steps.'

She swung her legs out of the car and stood up. The air was crisp and cool but it felt good to be outside. It had been over a week and a half since she'd last breathed fresh air. Her feet were still swollen but the pain was manageable if she could keep her legs elevated. It wasn't far to the house. She'd put her feet up again when she was inside. She knew she wasn't able to be a useful house guest, given that she couldn't stand for long, but she'd try not to be a nuisance.

Taking the stairs slowly and carefully, she entered through the front door, which opened directly into a large, open living space with the kitchen at one end. The floorboards were strewn with large rugs delineating the different spaces—living and dining—and the windows all looked out towards the lake. Enormous, overstuffed couches sat in front of a large stone fireplace in the living area.

The house was cool but there were plenty of blankets draped over the couches and fresh logs had been stacked in the fireplace grate, just waiting for someone to strike a match. Bookcases were built in on either side of the fireplace filled with books, board games, old vinyl records and jigsaw puzzles. Despite the fact that the house was now only used for holidays and weekend getaways, it had a welcoming feeling. Charli could imagine that Pat's childhood here had been a happy one.

She followed behind him as he gave her a brief tour. Behind the living room were several bedrooms and a couple of bathrooms. He put her bag in the room closest to the bathroom. The double bed in the centre was easily big enough for two but Charli noticed, with some disappointment, that he took his bag to a second room across the hall. Maybe that was just as well, she chided herself as Amy's warning replayed in her head. After all, she had sworn off relationships.

He boiled the kettle for tea and directed Charli to a chair set beside the fire. The chair was angled to look out over the view through the large windows down to the lake. A wooden jetty jutted out over the water and a rope swing hung in a gum tree near a fire pit.

'What is the name of the lake?' she asked.

'Lake Eildon.'

'It's beautiful. This must have been an incredible place to grow up.'

'It was brilliant. My brother and I had an adventurous childhood. Swimming, fishing, water-skiing in summer and snow-skiing in winter. Wombat Gully is only an hour away.'

'This is the brother who gave you that scar under your eye? Is he older or younger than you?'

'Three years younger.'

She sipped her tea. 'How long did you live here?'

'Until I was twelve. We moved to Melbourne when I started high school.'

'But your parents kept the house here?'

'We spent our holidays here. Summer and winter. I'm glad they kept it. I have fabulous memories of growing up here and I want Ella to have the opportunity to experience this lifestyle as well. It's harder now, being a single parent, but I have a lot of support from my parents.' Pat struck a match and Charli tried not to stare at his backside as the denim of his jeans stretched taut across it as he bent over to light the fire. 'Are you okay there for a bit?' he asked as he straightened up. 'I just want to chop some more wood.'

'I'm fine, thanks.' There was a pile of magazines on a small table beside her chair and Charli flicked through a couple as she drank her tea but her concentration was interrupted by the sound of Pat's axe splitting wood.

The view through the windows was incredible but Charli was restless. She'd been in the car for a few hours and cooped up in hospital for days before that. She'd had enough of being inside and on her own. She wanted to be outside. She wanted to be with Pat.

She grabbed her crutches and went out and sat on the veranda. Pat had his back to her and she watched, almost mesmerised, as he swung the axe. Despite the cool temperature of the day he had stripped off his shirt and the muscles in his back and arms were slick with sweat, gleaming in the late afternoon light. She watched his hands where they gripped the axe and remembered when he'd held her with those same hands. How warm they'd felt. How safe they'd made her feel.

He split the last log and started to throw the smaller pieces into a pile beside the fire pit. He turned and saw her watching him. He winked at her but didn't stop. Charli felt her nerves settle. She felt like this was where she was supposed to be. Here, with him.

Behind Pat she could see the sun starting to set over the lake. The mountains were growing grey in the shadows and the water was turning gold. It was still and peaceful. Sunset was rapidly becoming her favourite part of the day. On the edge of one of the paddocks, in the shadow of a stand of gum trees, she could see animals grazing.

'Are those sheep?'

'Where?'

'Over there.' She pointed at the animals whose shapes she could just make out in the dusky light. 'By the trees.'

'They're kangaroos.'

Charli stood up and leant on the veranda railing, as if the few extra inches would improve her sight. 'Kangaroos! I've never seen a live kangaroo before. Can we go closer?'

'They're wild,' he said with a laugh. 'They won't hang around.'

'They are so cute.'

'Don't judge a book by its cover,' he said as he tossed the last log onto the pile. 'They're a pest.'

'Really?'

'Yep. They destroy the crops and compete with the stock for feed,' he told her as he climbed the steps and leant against the veranda post.

He was standing close beside her. She could smell his sweat—warm, musky and masculine. She watched as he wiped himself down with his T-shirt and slung it over his shoulder. She couldn't keep her eyes off him and she had completely lost her train of thought.

She straightened up, bringing herself even closer to him. He was watching her watching him.

He bent his head and she saw his eyes darken. Her lips parted; he was close enough to kiss her.

His lips brushed her cheek and Charli closed her eyes in anticipation. She felt his hand on her hip, felt it curl around behind her and cup her buttock as he whispered into her ear, 'Hold that thought. I need a shower.'

She opened her eyes in time to see him smile at her before he turned and walked away, leaving her all hot and bothered and barely able to stand on shaky legs. She leant back against the railing as she tried to work out what had just happened. And what would happen next.

She heard water running as Pat turned the shower on. She could imagine him, stripped naked, hands soaping his chest, head tipped back under the spray as the warm water ran over his body. She could feel herself blushing and she shook her head. She hadn't realised she had such a vivid imagination. She needed something to keep her busy.

Charli moved into the kitchen and looked

in the fridge. Pat had said there was home-made soup for dinner. She ladled some into a pot and put it on the stove to reheat before putting bread rolls in the oven to warm.

She heard the shower stop as she ladled the soup into bowls and took the rolls from the oven. Dinner was ready but she couldn't manage to carry the food to the table while using crutches. She'd need Patrick's help.

She grabbed her crutches and hobbled into the passage to call him to the kitchen.

She rounded the corner and came face to face with Pat as he emerged from the bathroom.

Or rather, she came face to bare, muscular chest.

A few drops of water remained, glistening on his skin. He smelt of soap and she could feel the heat of the shower rising off him.

Without thinking, she lowered her gaze. He had a thick, fluffy, white towel wrapped around his hips and she knew he was naked beneath it.

Her heart was beating rapidly and she lifted her eyes and met his dark, intense gaze. She swallowed, suddenly and unexpectedly nervous, and swayed a little on her sore feet.

'Are you looking for me?' he asked as he reached for her, his large hands holding her by the arms as he steadied her. His hands were warm and gentle and her skin tingled under his touch.

'Dinner is ready,' she stammered.

One corner of his mouth twitched up in a smile. 'I might just put some clothes on.'

'Would you like some help?' The words passed her lips before she had time to think.

His smile widened. 'Do you think that's a good idea?'

Charli took a deep breath as she thought about what she was about to do. She nodded. 'I think it's a very good idea.'

His green eyes darkened and Charli caught her bottom lip between her teeth as she waited for his reply.

He bent his head and his words brushed over her cheek as he said, 'We won't be needing these then.' He eased the crutches away from her body and scooped her off her feet.

She wrapped her arms around his neck as he pressed her against his chest. She could feel his heart beating strong and fast against her. He was firm and hard in all the right places. She tilted her head and looked up at him. His lips were millimetres from hers. She licked her lips and watched as his pupils dilated. Her lips parted, a soft moan escaping her throat as he closed the gap and pressed his lips to hers. Her lips parted further as Pat's tongue slipped inside her mouth. She tightened her hold on him as she kissed him back. He tasted of mint, he tasted of desire and she couldn't remember ever wanting someone as badly as she wanted him.

His mouth broke from hers, leaving her lips swollen and lonely. 'Are you sure about this?'

She nodded. She was panting, out of breath, but she knew what she wanted. She wanted him. She wanted to taste him and feel him and let him take away the longing and the hunger that was eating away inside her and she couldn't think about anything else.

'I'm sure.'

She might have sworn off relationships but this could only be a fling anyway, this situation was only temporary. Besides, she was sure he was still in love with his late wife but she didn't care. It wasn't as though he could be unfaithful, neither was she trying to steal him away from Ella. What she wanted to do wouldn't affect anyone else, this was between the two of them, simply a physical relationship, not an emotional one. What was the harm in that?

Convinced there was none she made her final decision.

'I want you to make love to me.'

She didn't need to ask him twice.

CHAPTER EIGHT

HE PICKED HER up and she wrapped her legs around his waist as he carried her to his room. He kissed her as he walked. She had no idea how he negotiated the path but she didn't care. All she cared about was getting naked. All she cared about was finding out if the reality was going to be as good as her fantasies.

He sat on the bed and she nestled in his lap, her knees either side of his thighs. She slid her fingers into his hair. It was still damp and still unruly. She'd been wanting to touch his hair since the night she'd met him. She'd been wanting to do a lot of things. He was sexy and strong but gentle at the same time, and she had been longing to touch him for days.

She traced the scar under his eye with her thumb, lightly brushing the skin before letting her fingers move over his cheek and jaw. She ran her index finger over the ridges of his abdominal muscles, tracing them from where they began under his ribs, counting the bumps silently in her head, one, two, three, four, five…until they disappeared under the edge of the towel. Her fingers stilled and she saw him tense. He breathed out, a long slow breath.

She lifted her hand and placed it over his heart. She felt it beating, hard and fast. His nipples were hard and she ran her thumb over one brown nub and heard him catch his breath.

He didn't say a word but his hands spoke for him.

His right hand moved from her hip, sliding under her top. It was warm on her skin and as his thumb grazed the lace of her bra she felt her nipple tighten under his touch. He lifted the hem of her top and she raised her arms as he slid her clothes from her. With a flick of his fingers he undid her bra. He bent his head and she closed her eyes in ecstasy as his tongue licked her nipple before his mouth closed over her breast.

He flipped her over, off his lap and onto her back, and lifted her hips as he slid one hand under the waistband of her loose trousers. She wriggled out of her clothes until she lay almost naked before him.

He lay beside her, stretched out on the bed. His hand rested on her thigh. She parted her knees and his hand slid up the inside of her leg, sending spasms of desire through her. His fingers found the edges of her knickers, found the warmth of her centre, and Charli trembled as her desire intensified.

She watched as he ran his eyes over the length of her. His gaze was dark and intense. Her body was still varying shades of yellow and purple as the bruises faded but under his gaze she felt beautiful. Under the touch of his fingers she came alive.

His fingers were teasing and taunting her. She had to touch him. She put her hand on his knee and slid it under the towel. His erection was thick and firm and warm beneath her hand.

'I want you to make love to me,' she whispered. She needed him. She needed to feel his warmth, his energy.

'I don't want to hurt you.'

'You won't.'

He rolled over and opened a drawer beside the bed. She knew he was looking for protection. And hoped he found some. She wanted to be joined to him. Wanted him to bring her to orgasm.

She watched as he stood up and retrieved a small packet. She reached out and flicked the towel from his waist. He was now completely naked and Charli couldn't take her eyes off him. He was glorious. Perfect.

She took her knickers off as he sheathed himself. He stood and watched her. Waiting. She bent her knees and spread her legs further, letting him see, inviting him in.

His dark eyes met hers as she reached for him, wrapping her hand around his length. 'I want you inside me.'

He moaned and removed her hand as he knelt on the bed. He held both of hers in his and pinned them above her head. He moved between her thighs and bent his head and it was her turn to moan as he covered one breast with his lips, sucking on her swollen nipple as he thrust into her.

Charli pushed up, arching her hips and back as he entered her, wanting, needing to take all of him in. She welcomed him in and let him fill her. Physically and emotionally he sated her. She was no longer an individual, she was no longer abandoned. He filled her physically and emotionally as she let him possess her.

She dissolved into a state of absolute pleasure. There was no room for any of the thoughts that had been swirling in her head for days. There was no time to think about what had happened, to her or to Pat. There was just the two of them at this moment. Together. Entwined. She wasn't going to think about the past or the future. There was only the present and she was going to make the most of the moment she'd been given. She was going to enjoy the man in her bed.

She woke to the sound of kookaburras laughing as the sun streamed in the window. She was alone in the bed but there was a note on the table beside her, tucked under a mug of tea. She picked up the mug, surprised to find it was still warm, and read the note.

Pat had gone fishing and hadn't wanted to wake her.

Had he needed time alone with his thoughts?

Did she need to be alone with hers?

She'd followed her heart last night, followed her desire, and she didn't regret it. Not yet. Pat was not a good match for her long term, she had no intention of getting seriously involved with a single father, no intention of being cast in the role of stepmother, but that didn't need to stop her from having some fun for the next couple of days. It wasn't like they could have a long-term future. She had to go back to the UK at some point as she was due to start work and further training in less than a month. But this could be fun for a couple of days.

She showered and dressed while she relived the events of last night in her head. She smiled as she hugged her thoughts to herself. She had never really expected reality to outdo her fantasies but she was happy to discover she'd been proved wrong. Last night had been everything she'd dreamt of and more, and for the first time since the landslide she felt happy, relaxed and peaceful.

She scanned the shore of the lake, looking for Pat. The banks were empty and there was no one on the jetty. Had he gone out in a boat? Did he have a boat? Her heart skittered anxiously until she reminded herself that he had grown up here. He knew the area and the lake. He wouldn't have put himself in danger.

A fire glowed in the fireplace, Pat must have lit it before he'd gone out. Charli threw another log on to keep it burning while she settled down with a cup of tea and a book. She had one eye on the story and the other trained on the lake. Watching and waiting for Pat.

Eventually she heard an engine and saw a boat approach and tie up to the jetty. She watched as Pat leapt ashore, carrying a bucket.

'Good morning,' he greeted her as he stepped into the house. He was smiling and looked relaxed, and only then did she realise she'd been a little uncertain. Unsure of how he would be feeling today. 'Do you fancy fish for lunch?' he asked as he opened the fridge door.

'That sounds good.'

'And how do you feel about fishermen? Do you fancy them too?'

She grinned. 'I find the local fishermen irresistible.'

'Is that so?' he said as he came and leant over her sofa. 'Just how many do you know?'

'Only one but he's more than enough for me.' She reached up and grabbed a fistful of the soft, grey cable-knit sweater he was wearing and pulled him down to her.

He kissed her firmly on the lips. 'No regrets about last night then?'

'Of course not. Why?'

He squeezed in behind her on the sofa and pulled her back until she was lying against his chest. She could hear the beat of his heart under her ear. She snuggled in closer as he wrapped one arm around her shoulders. 'I was worried that I'd taken advantage of you.'

She laughed. 'I think you know I was more than willing. I have wanted you since the moment I first saw you and, even with everything that has happened since I met you in the bar, that hasn't changed. I'm a big girl, Pat, I make my own decisions.'

'Are you sure?'

'I'm positive.'

'I promised I had honourable intentions and the next thing you know I've got you naked in my bed. I wanted to help you. I wanted to give you time to recover. To heal. I thought you needed to escape, not just from the hospital and the media attention but from the world in a way.'

'And that is exactly what you are doing.

Let's not over-think it, let's just enjoy the next few days. And each other. We can both re-charge and be ready to get on with our lives when the time comes. I don't want to think. I want to feel. Last night was incredible. Shall we see if we can repeat it before lunch?' she whispered.

Charli arched her back as he slid his hand under her sweater. She felt her nipple harden in response to his touch and then there was no room in her mind for anything other than Pat.

Charli spent the next two days in a quiet bub-ble. She slept and read while Pat fished and did some minor repairs to the house. They shared wine and food by the fire and at night they shared a bed. They didn't discuss the outside world. For forty-eight hours it ceased to exist, and Charli was content just to be in the moment, away from the real world. She knew it was out there, waiting, but she was happy not to think about it for now.

On the last night they sat by the fire pit, bundled in thick jackets and blankets under the dark sky. She lay in Pat's arms as they shared a bottle of wine and looked at the stars. 'It's so beautiful. I wondered if I'd ever see the stars again when I was trapped. But I don't recognise these ones, your stars are so different.'

'Does it feel strange, lying under a different sky?' he asked.

'It feels like a dream.' She felt safe and comfortable in his arms and she could almost let herself believe that this was exactly where she was meant to be, even though she knew it couldn't last. 'It's almost impossible to imagine that in a few weeks' time I'll be back in London.'

'Are you ready to go back?'

'Yes.' And, no, she thought, but she didn't have an option. 'I've worked really hard to get into the GP training program, I need to get back. I need to be busy. I need to move forward.'

Going home was the safe option. She had a job, a career, a life waiting for her there. She knew she would take the safe option. What other choice did she have? She couldn't throw all of that away on the chance that Pat might be ready to move on. She wanted to be important to someone, she wanted to be special, and he'd made it clear that he wasn't looking for anyone special.

From the beginning their time together had been limited and while she could daydream about staying, it was only a fantasy. He had a daughter who needed his attention, one she was unlikely even to meet, and she wasn't sure she wanted to. That would be a dose of reality that she wasn't equipped to deal with. She was happy here, secluded in their own little world, and she wasn't naïve enough to think they could take what they had here back into their normal lives. Sexual chemistry wasn't enough to build something lasting on.

She would go home with her memories but, meanwhile, she would enjoy the last few hours with him. She'd made a decision to focus on her career but that didn't preclude her from enjoying this time with him. She wanted this interlude, a chance to restore some peace in her heart, even though she knew it couldn't last. Not the peace or the time with Pat. They both had complicated lives and she couldn't stay. Relationships didn't work out for her. She was always left alone. And she wasn't going to keep making the same mistakes. She would take pleasure in his company for as long as they had and then she would leave.

It was time to return to reality. They were headed back to Melbourne and the closer they got to the city the more Charli felt as though time was running out. They hadn't talked about what came next. She didn't want to be the one to raise the topic but it was becoming increasingly obvious as the kilometres ticked over that she would have to.

'Can you recommend a good hotel for me once we get back to the city?' she asked.

'A hotel? What for?'

'I need somewhere to stay. My review at the hospital is still several days away and I can't fly until then.'

'I thought you'd stay with me.'

'At your house?'

'Yes.'

'With you and Ella?'

'Yes. Is there a problem?'

'Does she know about me?'

'No.'

Pat had spoken to his daughter each day while they'd stayed at the lake. He hadn't tried to take the calls privately and Charli had been able to hear most of the conversation. She hadn't heard her name mentioned once and it had reinforced that Pat also had a different reality waiting for him when they left the lake house. He had responsibilities, not just to his career but to his daughter. Charli wasn't interested in playing happy families, she didn't know how to.

'So she'll come home to find a random stranger staying her house and you think she'll be okay with that?'

He'd told her that he had to think carefully about how his actions would impact on Ella. Was he ignoring his own advice now?

'She's three, Charli, her world revolves around her.'

'And your parents? What about them?'

'I have a spare room. You can stay in there for appearances' sake if you're worried.'

Perhaps he wasn't asking, or expecting, her to play happy families. He seemed quite content with his life the way it was.

Was this the end? She was under no illusion that things could continue between them long term but she hadn't actually thought about the end. She wished they could have stayed hidden away on the shores of the lake but that wasn't reality. For either of them.

'I'm not collecting Ella until after dinner tonight,' he said. 'It'll take us a few hours to get back to Melbourne. Why don't you think about it?'

'All right, I— Oh, my God! Stop. *Stop!*'

Charli flung her hands into the air and screamed as she watched helplessly as an accident unfolded before her. She'd seen the driver of a parked car open his door just as a cyclist was passing. The cyclist swerved to avoid the door but veered into the path of the car in front of Pat's.

Pat slammed on his brakes as the car in front of him swerved suddenly, and although Pat was able to avoid a collision the cyclist wasn't so fortunate. They watched, horrified, as the cyclist hit the bonnet of the car in front and bounced off the windscreen.

Pat switched off the engine, hit his hazard lights and leapt from the car. 'Check the driver,' he said to Charli as he ran towards the cyclist, who was now lying prostrate on the road.

Charli limped to the car in front. She didn't bother to grab her crutches, she was in too much of a hurry. The driver, an elderly gentleman, was conscious but obviously shaken.

'He rode right into me! I didn't have time to stop.'

'I know, I saw it happen,' she said as calmly as possible. 'Are you all right?'

'I think so.'

'I'm a doctor. Do you think you can walk? I can help you out of the car.'

His windscreen was smashed so a tow-truck would need to be called, and Charli knew the ambulance officers would want to check him out and give him the all clear.

She could hear Pat issuing instructions to other bystanders. Getting one to call an ambulance and another to direct traffic. The driver appeared to be okay and Charli knew Pat could probably use some help, but she needed to take care of the elderly man first.

'Do you have any medical conditions I should know about?' she asked as she helped him to the footpath.

'I'm on medication for my blood pressure and arthritis.'

There was a bus stop nearby and Charli assisted him to the seat. His knees shook as he sat down and Charli looked at him with some concern as his face went slightly grey.

'Are you feeling okay?'

He was rubbing his left shoulder with his hand. 'I think I might have strained my shoulder,' he said. His voice was breathless and, looking at him, Charli knew it was more than that.

He was having a heart attack.

'Pat!' she called. 'I need some help here!'

She caught the man as he toppled forward off the seat. She laid him on the ground and felt for a pulse. It disappeared under her fingers.

She started CPR.

Out of the corner of her eye she saw Pat run back to his car and when he got to her he had a resuscitation mask in his hand. He knelt beside her and Charli nodded, letting him know she needed him to breathe for the man. She counted out loud as Pat positioned the mask and pinched the man's nose. 'Twenty-eight, twenty-nine, thirty.'

She took a break as Pat breathed into the man's mouth.

He did two breaths and then sat back as Charli resumed compressions.

'Are you still on the phone to the ambulance?' Charli heard him ask one of the bystanders. 'Can you tell them it is now a category one, we have a patient in cardiac arrest.'

Charli and Pat continued CPR, alternating roles, until the paramedics arrived to take over. They hadn't managed to resuscitate the driver and Charli didn't like the ambulance officers' chances either. She had no idea how much time had passed but it had felt like many minutes.

She hobbled to Pat's car and collapsed into the passenger seat while Pat gave the crews a summary of the event. Eventually the two ambulances left the scene with their lights flashing and sirens screaming, and Pat joined her in the car.

'How was the cyclist?' she asked.

'He's pretty banged up,' he said as he pulled into the traffic, which was now heavily congested. 'He has a few broken bones, possibly a fractured scapula, collarbone, ribs and pelvis but it's internal injuries we were worried about. How are you?'

Charli was exhausted and her feet were sore. Kneeling on a hard footpath hadn't done them any favours and she suspected her efforts had all been in vain. 'Tired, and my feet are sore, but I'm in a lot better shape than either of those two.'

'This traffic is going to hold us up now. If you're in pain I think you should stay with me, at least for tonight. It'll be late before we get back to the city anyway. If you want to go to a hotel tomorrow, I'll sort something out then.'

Charli hesitated. She hadn't decided what to do and she was now too tired to think about it. She hesitated, but not for long. What would be the harm in staying with Pat for one more night?

Charli wandered through the house while Pat went to collect his daughter. She'd expected something comfortable and cosy, like the house in the country, but the house was sleek and modern. It didn't feel like Pat. She assumed his late wife had decorated it but she wondered what he'd changed in the past two years. She almost expected his wife to walk into the room, her presence was still so evident. Had Pat deliberately chosen not to change anything? Was this his way of keeping her memory alive?

Photos of Ella and of Margie with Ella dominated the shelves. Charli felt like an intruder as she picked up some framed photos but she couldn't resist. Ella was gorgeous. She had Pat's colouring, green eyes and dark hair, but her hair was a mass of ringlets and her face was a miniature version of her mother's. Margie was also dark with eyes that were bright with life and a smile that was full of laughter. They looked like they'd been happy.

She sighed as she replaced the photos. It was blindingly obvious that Pat was not ready to let go of his past.

She went to the pantry and searched for the tea, having decided she'd put the kettle on and take a cup of tea to her room. She probably should get off her feet and tea always made everything slightly more bearable.

Charli was still in the kitchen when Pat arrived home with Ella. She hadn't been able to decide where she should be. Hadn't decided how she was going to deal with meeting his daughter. Pat had assured her that Ella wouldn't have a problem with Charli staying. She was sociable child, used to being surrounded by lots of different people. He'd told her that he wouldn't have invited Charli to stay if he'd thought it would cause problems, but Charli was starting to feel uncomfortable now, although she had enough insight into herself to realise that her fears were based on her recollections of her own childhood and had nothing to do with Ella.

She took a deep breath as Pat came into the kitchen, carrying his daughter. She was overthinking things, there was no need to be nervous.

Pat set Ella down.

He rested his hand on top of Ella's dark curls. 'Ella, this is my friend, Charli. She's going to stay with us for a while.'

Ella stayed close to his side but looked up at Charli with her green eyes that mirrored Pat's, and Charli's nerves returned with a vengeance.

'Hello, Ella,' she managed to say. She wondered what she was supposed to do next. Should she squat down, bring herself closer to Ella's level, or would that be too confronting? She didn't know what to do so she stayed put, almost frozen in the corner of the kitchen.

'Remember, before you were born, Mummy and I lived in England?' Pat talked to fill the silence. 'Charli is from England.'

'Did you know my mummy?'

'No.' Charli shook her head.

Ella was looking at Charli's heavily bandaged feet. 'What happened to your feet?'

'I was in an accident.'

'My mummy was in an accident. She's in heaven now.'

'My mum is in heaven too.'

'Do you think they are friends?'

'I don't know.' Charli felt uncomfortable. She hadn't expected to be having this conversation with a three-year-old and had no idea how to respond.

Her phone vibrated and she snatched it off the countertop, relieved to have something to divert her attention. 'Can you excuse me, please?' she said as she left the room.

Pat watched her go, wondering what the hell had just happened.

That hadn't gone at all well.

Why was she so uncomfortable?

His parents-in-law had bathed and fed Ella before he'd collected her so he started her bedtime routine while Charli was on the phone. He helped Ella to clean her teeth and left her to choose a story while he went to speak to Charli to find out what was wrong.

Charli had finished on the phone but she spoke before he had a chance to.

'Can I talk to you?' she asked, and continued when he nodded. 'That was Harriet. The television stations are still calling, wanting to interview me.'

'We've had calls to Special Ops too.'

'You have? Why haven't you said something?'

'The journalists are only interested in an interview with us if they can interview you too. I told Connor you weren't keen, so he's shut them down.'

'Do you think they'll give up?'

'Eventually. Something else will come along that's more newsworthy.'

'If I agreed to give just one interview, do you think they would they be happy with that?'

'If you made it clear that's all you were prepared to do, I think that could work. Are you thinking about it?'

Charli nodded. 'Do you have a PR division as part of Special Ops?'

'We have a media liaison officer in the ambulance service. Why?'

'If the reporters were interviewing one of your team as well, do you think the media person could set it all up? I wouldn't know what to do.'

'I'm sure they could.'

'Would you do the interview with me?'

'Me?'

She nodded. 'I'd feel better if we could do it together. Do you think that would be a possibility or does the ambulance service have a regular spokesperson?'

Pat shook his head. 'Any one of us can give interviews. Sometimes we're briefed and sometimes it's on the spot at a scene. It should be possible to organise. I've got to read to Ella but I can make some calls after that. Unless you want to read to her?'

Maybe that could help break the ice. He hadn't expected Charli to be so reticent. Everyone loved Ella and he couldn't begin to fathom what the problem was.

'Me?'

He nodded.

Charli looked terrified. 'Can't you just ask tomorrow when you go to work?'

'I may not get time. Work can be a bit unpredictable, as I'm sure you can imagine. It's easier to do it now.' He felt a little bit guilty. Charli was obviously reluctant to read to Ella but he couldn't understand why. 'She's choosing the story now.'

Charli still hesitated. Maybe he shouldn't have pushed her but it was too late now.

'I don't think I can,' she said.

'Why not?'

'I'm no good with children. I don't know what to do. What if I do or say the wrong thing?'

'It's a story, Charli, all you have to do is read it.'

Finally, she nodded.

CHAPTER NINE

CHARLI HAD READ to Ella on the first night, thinking it was best to get it over and done with and knowing that, as Pat was doing her a favour, she needed to do one in return, but she hadn't counted on being asked to read *every* night. She had debated the wisdom of staying at Pat's but since Amy had returned to Wombat Gully her only other option, until she was fit to fly, was to book alternative accommodation, which would mean being on her own. She really *hated* being alone, so she'd stayed.

She been there for five nights and it was becoming harder and harder to maintain a safe distance.

Ella's favourite book was *Paddington*. Charli had loved that book too as a child and reading wasn't a problem, but spending this one-on-one time with Ella was. She was adorable, warm and open, and secure in the knowledge that she was loved, she had not hesitated to welcome Charli into her life.

But her open manner scared Charli. She didn't want to get attached to Ella, she didn't want to disappoint her. She knew she needed to maintain some distance, and didn't want to get too close or too comfortable, knowing it would make it more difficult when she had to leave. And she knew she couldn't stay. This couldn't be her life. She couldn't get too attached, to Ella or to Pat. It wasn't fair on any of them.

But Pat, or more accurately, Ella, seemed determined to include her in their lives and the more time Charli spent with them the harder it was to stay removed. She could feel herself being drawn in. They made her feel safe and secure. She was starting to feel like she was a part of a family and the feeling was addictive. It was what she had always wanted but was afraid of at the same time. She knew that loving people left her open to heartbreak.

But even knowing the risks, she couldn't avoid spending time with Pat and his daughter. If she was completely honest, she didn't *want* to avoid it. She had no issue with spending time with Pat behind closed doors but she was glad he hadn't suggested that she meet his parents or his friends. She didn't want to get more involved in his life as it would only make it harder to leave, but getting close to Ella was a different thing altogether and she was trying to limit the time she spent with her. Some things, however, she discovered, were not negotiable, which was exactly how she found herself agreeing to spend a day at the zoo with Pat and his daughter.

She'd tried half-heartedly to get out of the excursion, claiming that it would be too much walking, but Pat had insisted. Apparently the zoo had wheelchairs and he was happy to push her. She'd then tried to suggest that he might like the time alone with Ella but Ella was as insistent as her father and now here they were, all three of them, at the entrance gate.

'Where shall we go first, Ella?' Pat asked as he paid the admission fee. He knew what Ella's answer would be—it was always the same.

'The Butterfly House.'

Kept at a constant twenty-eight degrees, the butterfly exhibit was the perfect spot on a grey and drizzly Melbourne day, and Ella skipped ahead as Pat pushed Charli's wheelchair through the zoo. He and Ella had finally persuaded Charli to accompany them and he had a surprise organised for later in the morning but, knowing Ella's preferences, he'd allowed time for the butterflies first.

Charli had stopped looking so afraid when she was spending time with Ella but he hadn't been certain she would agree to spend the day with them doing one of Ella's favourite activities. He knew she was still holding back, fearful of engaging fully with Ella. It was odd. He'd thought she'd feel empathy with his daughter as they'd both suffered the same tragedy of losing their mothers at a young age but Charli seemed reluctant to get too close.

Maybe that wasn't a bad thing because she was only going to be in their lives for a short time, but if he'd thought for one moment that having Charli with them would have been at all disruptive for Ella, he wouldn't have suggested it. Ella was resilient and she enjoyed Charli's company like she enjoyed everyone's. When Charli left, Ella would have plenty of other people to fill that void so he hadn't thought it would be a problem. At least, not for Ella. But he'd come to realise that *he* would be the one who would be most affected when Charli left. He would be the one who missed her. Ella would move on, she was better at that than he was.

Charli had none of the same reservations about spending time with him, though, but she had insisted that they keep their relationship behind closed doors. Neither Ella nor his parents were allowed to know just what was happening between them but that was okay. Ella went to bed early and that gave him and Charli hours alone together.

But spending this time with her was complicating his feelings. He enjoyed spending time with her, physically and intellectually she stimulated him. He'd been attracted to her from the first moment and he'd been keen to pursue a physical relationship but he hadn't expected to connect any more deeply than that. He'd thought they could have some time together and then happily go their separate ways, but he liked having her in his life. He just wasn't sure how, or if, she could fit more permanently.

Did he want to go there?

She had a life in England, a career, and he

had a life here, a career, a family, a daughter. Neither of them could give those things up. Timing was everything and he had a feeling their timing was wrong. It was too soon.

He couldn't worry about it now, he decided as he pushed Charli's chair through the double doors into the butterfly house. He'd enjoy the day and pretend he knew what he was doing.

'Sit very still, Charli,' Ella instructed, and Pat stifled a laugh. It was one thing for Ella to issue commands but quite another for her to follow her own rules. She danced from foot to foot and watched the butterflies. There were hundreds of them, looking like rose petals swirling in the breeze.

'Pretend you're a tree, Ella,' he said in an effort to get her to stand still. She stuck her arms out but continued to shuffle excitedly. Eventually the butterflies stopped fluttering and dipping and one landed on Ella's finger, to be quickly and unceremoniously frightened away when Ella's attention was caught by something else.

'Charli! You've got a butterfly on your

head! Daddy, take a photo,' Ella ordered, used to having everything captured on his phone.

Charli had a butterfly perched on her head like an ornament. She was smiling at him as he took the photo and his breath caught in his throat and his chest went tight with desire. Another butterfly landed on her shoulder and he took a second photo.

'They like you, Charli!' Ella chattered. 'I think it's because you smell nice. Doesn't she smell nice, Daddy?'

He bent his head and smelt her hair. 'She does indeed, Ella.' Charli was blushing but her eyes were shining as he straightened up and looked at her.

'Maybe they like my hand cream.' She rummaged in her handbag and pulled out the tube. 'Why don't we put some on you, Ella?'

It was the first time in Pat's experience that Charli had voluntarily connected with Ella. Maybe she was getting under Charli's defences. He figured that her reluctance to get attached to Ella stemmed from her own childhood but Ella was irresistible and he didn't think it would do Charli any harm to spend time with her.

Charli rubbed cream into Ella's hands before dabbing a bit on the end of Ella's nose. Much to Ella's delight, a butterfly landed on her nose and Pat knew Charli had made a friend for life out of his daughter now. All that remained was to see how Charli felt about Ella.

They watched the butterflies feeding at the nectar tables until the glasshouse began to fill with people and Ella began to get restless. He pushed Charli out past the elephants to the platypus pool, where they laughed at the curious creature as it dived and twisted in a display of underwater acrobatics before they wandered through the Australian animal section to the kangaroo enclosure.

In typical Melbourne fashion, the sun had finally decided to make an appearance, pushing weakly through the clouds, but it was enough for the kangaroos to seek out the warm spots and lie basking in the sun.

People were milling around the enclosure as Pat parked Charli's chair near the gate and locked the brakes. 'We need to leave your wheelchair here.'

'What for?'

'We can't take it into the enclosure.'

'We're going in?' He nodded. 'With the kangaroos?'

'If you want to feed them you need to go in. They don't make a habit of letting them out.' He smiled.

Charli's blue eyes lit up. 'We can go in and feed them? Really?'

'Really.' This was the surprise he'd organised. He'd paid extra for the experience but he hadn't been able to resist. 'And pat them.'

Charli was out of the chair before Pat finished his sentence.

'That is amazing, thank you.' She flung her arms around his neck and kissed him on the cheek, possibly forgetting her own rules, but she'd dropped her arms almost before he'd registered her hug and held her hand out to Ella. 'Let's go.'

They listened quietly as the keeper gave a quick safety briefing, reminding visitors not to run or chase the kangaroos. 'Find a spot to sit quietly and let the kangaroos come to you. They are used to being hand fed, they'll be eager. Take some pellets and hold your hand flat, they'll eat off your hand.' She showed them how to hold their hands and then passed out small bags of pellets.

Charli and Ella chose a log to sit on. They sat side by side as the kangaroos fed from their hands. Pat took several photos as they fed and patted the kangaroos.

'They feel like velvet!' Charli exclaimed, as a young joey nuzzled her hand.

The joey turned and dived back into its mother's pouch, legs akimbo, and Ella giggled.

'Isn't it a bit big to be in the pouch?' Charli asked at the sight of its hind legs sticking out.

'They stay in the pouch for about six months,' the keeper said, 'but continue to go in and out of the pouch until they are almost a year old.'

Charli shook her head as she fed the mother and laughed along with Ella. Pat watched them together with a vision of what his life could be like with someone to share it with.

'Thank you, Pat, this is incredible.' Charli looked up and smiled at him and his heart skipped a beat and he knew, right then, that he was starting to fall for her.

'It's my pleasure,' he said, then pretended to check his phone. He didn't want her to be able to read his expression. He was terrified she would see what he was thinking and that it would scare her. He sensed it would be too much too soon for her.

'My food's all gone,' Ella said as she up-ended the bag to prove her point.

'Mine too,' Charli said. She took both bags and they had one final pat before they were ushered out of the enclosure.

'I want to be a baby joey. Can I sit on your lap, Charli?'

Charli held her arms out and Ella clambered onto her lap. She curled herself into a ball and snuggled in. Charli tucked her coat around her, creating a makeshift pouch.

Back at the house Pat put a movie on the television and Charli and Ella fell asleep together on the couch. Ella had insisted on continuing with her joey impersonation and had refused to leave Charli's side. She lay curled up with her head on Charli's lap and Charli's arm was draped over her, holding her close. It was the most relaxed he had seen her with his daughter. Perhaps, with time, this could work out for all of them.

Charli barely recognised the face staring back at her from the mirror in front of the make-up chair. She hadn't expected the television station to bother with her make-up but now she was shocked to see that her bruises, which had been fading, had been accentuated by the make-up artist. She looked more battered than she had in days. Was that the effect they wanted?

She leaned in towards the mirror as the artist removed the white collar that had protected her clothes and started to clean the brushes.

Charli spun around in the chair, about to stand, when the door opened and Pat stuck his head into the room.

'All good?' he asked, before she saw him do a slight double take.

He crossed the room, coming closer. He put his fingers under her chin and Charli felt the now familiar frisson of desire with his touch, but that was quickly wiped out by Pat's frown. She knew what he was thinking.

'I was expecting to look better than I do in real life, not worse,' she said, trying to remain positive and make light of the situation.

'You're still gorgeous, but...' he turned her face to the side, examining the end result '...you look like you've gone three rounds with a prize fighter. I hope no one thinks I've done that to you.'

'I'm not sure why they've emphasised my bruises. What angle do you think they're going with?' She was growing more nervous by the minute and worried about what questions might be asked and how she would manage.

She'd agreed to the interview on the condition that Pat would do it with her, and she'd expected they would be interviewed together. She wanted to do the entire interview with Pat beside her but the producers, and Stacey, the show's host, had decided Pat would join in later. They felt it would be more dramatic.

She knew she was relying on Pat more than was healthy. It was so easy to let him take charge, to let him make the decisions. She didn't want to face up to the real world yet and suddenly she wondered if the interview was about to make her. Would she have to relive the entire disaster? She could feel her heart rate quicken and her breathing become more rapid. She reached for some paper towel to wipe her sweaty hands.

Things weren't going quite the way she'd expected.

'It will be okay,' Pat reassured her. 'Take your time answering the questions, there's no need to hurry. Take some deep breaths now,' he said as the door opened again and an assistant came to collect Charli. 'I'll be with you as soon as I can.'

Charli was escorted into the studio during an ad break. The interview was being broadcast live, which was something else she hadn't anticipated. She really hoped she didn't make a fool of herself.

A microphone was clipped to her collar and a battery pack tucked into her pocket before she was settled into position on a very small couch opposite the journalist, Stacey, who was in a chair. Fortunately, Charli was allowed to be seated when the interview began and didn't have to make her way to the couch using her crutches, although they had been propped next to the couch for effect.

Now that she was on set, under the glare of the lights and with no familiar faces, she wished she'd stood her ground. She could have done with Pat's moral support. She hoped the first part of the interview would be over quickly and then he would be with her.

She took a deep breath when she heard the

producer start the countdown to the end of the ad break and mentally prepared herself as Stacey began the introductions.

'Here with me today I have Charlotte Lawson, the sole survivor of the Wombat Gully landslide that claimed the lives of fifteen people earlier this month. Welcome to the programme, Charlotte.'

Stacey's dark hair was styled and sprayed with hairspray, not a strand out of place. Her forehead was Botoxed and her lips plump. Charli found it quite disconcerting being interviewed by someone whose face was devoid of all expression. She wished she could tell what Stacey was thinking.

There was a large digital screen to Charli's left, positioned at the back of the studio, and on it Charli could see a photograph of Wombat Gully Resort with the big brown scar on the landscape and the rubble of the ruined buildings strewn down the mountain. She turned back to face Stacey.

'You were trapped, buried alive, for almost forty hours. You must have been terrified.'

She should have known the interview would go for drama and sensationalism. She'd watched enough of these interviews herself over the years. But, despite the dramatics, Stacey was right. Charli had been afraid.

'I was. I can't remember ever feeling so afraid. So alone.'

'Can you describe it to us?'

'It's hard to describe. It was so dark. Pitch black. I couldn't see anything. I had no idea what had happened, where anything was. Water flooded the floor and dripped through the roof. I could smell sewage. It was freezing cold. I was breathing in dust—it was so thick I thought it would choke me—and I was afraid I might run out of air. I tried calling out but no one responded.'

'Did you ever imagine that you might not be found?'

'Yes.' That had been her overriding fear. That she would die in a tomb, alone.

'How did you deal with that?'

'One step at a time. I was cold and thirsty and tired and that made it difficult to focus, to work out what to do. I tried to stay warm. I knew hypothermia and dehydration were the biggest dangers. There was nothing to drink. I tried not to move too much but I had to make noise, I had to try to get someone's attention.'

'And how did you do that?'

'I found a metal pole and when I could hear people nearby I'd hit it against the bed frame—but then everything would go quiet and I thought people were taking a break. I didn't know if they'd ever hear me.'

'But, in fact,' Stacey said, 'the rescuers called for quiet on the site so they could listen for noise, for a sound that might indicate there were survivors. They were, in fact, listening for you.'

'Yes. I had no idea I was working at cross-purposes to them. I was lucky to be found.'

'Yes, you were the lucky one. You were found by Patrick Reeves, one of a team of Special Operations paramedics, and he joins us now too. Wouldn't we all love to be rescued by someone tall, dark and handsome?' Stacey said as she turned to the side of the studio and watched as Pat came into view. 'Welcome, Pat. You're the hero in this story.' She stood up to shake Pat's hand and Charli could see the introduction embarrassed him.

'I was just one of hundreds of people searching the area,' he said as he sat beside Charli on the tiny couch.

'But you were the one who heard Charli's cry for help,' Stacey said, ramping up the melodrama. 'How did you feel? Talk us through the moment when you heard her voice.'

'I thought I was hearing things. I thought my imagination was working overtime initially. We'd been working hard in tough conditions, getting nowhere, and we were starting to think we wouldn't find *any* survivors. When I realised I hadn't imagined the noise, it was a huge relief.'

'And, Charli, that must have been a miraculous moment for you. Making contact. It's incredible to think that you could come through almost unscathed when there were no other survivors. Have you seen that before, Pat? You've been to lots of disasters. You've risked your life time and again.'

Visions flashed up on the large screen to Charli's left. The image of Wombat Gully Resort was replaced by photos of other tragedies. Charli knew the viewers would be able to see it. She could pick out Pat in a few of the photos, not all, there were a lot of media shots, but Stacey was talking about Pat's role in these other events—a train derailment in the Dandenong Ranges, some school students lost in the bush on an overnight hike, an air-lift from a skiing accident.

'It's unusual to have only one survivor with something of this scale,' Pat admitted.

'And you were at the resort for a training exercise. Were you training for a landslide?'

'Not as such, but the processes are the same in any disaster.'

'Had you ever been involved in anything of this magnitude?'

'No. And I hope I never am again. We're in the business of saving lives and losing so many people was awful. It was an enormous tragedy.'

Charli knew he was thinking about the people he hadn't saved, the ones he'd heard calling for help minutes after the disaster, the ones who he'd known had survived the initial landslide only to perish from their injuries or from the elements before they could be rescued.

'But saving Charli must have given everyone hope.'

'It was unbelievable.'

The image on the screen changed again and a photo of Charli being lifted from the rubble appeared. She was strapped to the spinal board, filthy and dishevelled, but the setting sun cast a golden light onto her. Pat could be seen leaning over her and her eyes were fixed on him.

'Tell us what you were thinking in this moment, Charli.'

Charli remembered that moment vividly. She remembered not wanting to let Pat out of her sight but that revelation felt much too personal to share on national television. 'I was just so glad to see the sky. I was so relieved to be out of there and the sunset was spectacular.'

'Pat, do you think there was a reason Charli survived?'

'A reason?'

'Yes. Do you think this experience has brought you closer? Have you forged a relationship that will endure into the future? I hear you were a frequent visitor while Charli was in hospital. That's not normal practice for first responders or emergency personnel, is it? It's obvious there's a connection between you. Are you single? What about *you*, Charli, are you single?'

Charli wasn't sure where Stacey was going with this angle. She was completely unprepared for the question and she could only assume Pat was too.

'Oh, I've put you on the spot,' Stacey said. 'You're blushing, Charli. Is there more to the story? An addition to the happy ending?'

Charli realised, too late, that it had been a mistake to ask Pat to do the interview with her. Someone had obviously done their homework. She had no idea who Stacey had spoken to or who had done the digging, but the interview was taking a turn that she wasn't prepared for. Stacey was definitely going for drama but not in the direction Charli had expected.

She was suddenly aware of how close she and Pat were sitting. They had no choice on such a small couch but she wondered how it looked to the viewers. She didn't want to be the topic of rumours and innuendo. She shook her head. 'No, there's no more to the story.'

'You left hospital with Patrick on your discharge, though, didn't you?'

How on earth did she know that? Charli was afraid to ask, she didn't think she wanted to hear the answer.

Pat answered the question with one of his

own. 'Charli is a visitor who lost everything in the landslide. Where was she supposed to go?'

Pat didn't sound as though he was going to admit to their relationship. And neither was she.

'To her sister's, perhaps?' Stacey said, before changing tack. 'I understand you're a widower, Pat, a single dad. It was interesting that Charli chose to go with you.'

'Interesting to whom?' Pat sounded annoyed now. 'Amy is back in Wombat Gully. Did you expect Charli to return there after everything that had happened?'

'No, not at all. I think everyone is curious about what happens next, though. That photo looks like the start of something to me and I'm sure everyone would love a fairy-tale ending to the tragedy. Charli?' Stacey was not backing down quietly.

'I think they're going to be disappointed,' she replied. 'I don't live here and when I am able to fly I will be going back to England.'

Charli loved the idea of fairy-tale endings as much as anybody but despite finding herself imagining a life with Patrick and Ella she knew it was impossible. She might love the idea of happily-ever-after but Patrick hadn't made any suggestions that he was feeling as though there could be a future for the two of them.

His house was still full of Margie's photos and Margie's touches. Charli was under no illusion that he was thinking about anything permanent. She needed to be careful. She couldn't afford to get in any deeper, to give her heart away completely. She would be leaving and she wanted her heart intact when she went. Giving it away twice, to Patrick and to Ella, would only cause her twice as much pain when she returned to the UK.

'There's nothing that would convince you to stay. A new romance, perhaps?'

Charli shook her head and Stacey turned to Pat. 'What about you, Pat?' Charli held her breath, waiting to hear if Pat would share his thoughts about her plans. Would he say he'd like her to stay?

But Stacey didn't ask him the question Charli hoped for. 'Is there anyone special in your life?'

'Only my daughter.'

Pain pierced Charli's chest at the implications of Pat's words. She knew Ella came first in Pat's life, that was fair and right, and she suspected that she was also further down the list than his late wife, but to hear Pat neglect to mention her at all was hurtful.

Pat's tone suggested that he wouldn't be answering any more questions and Charli was relieved when Stacey ended the interview. She was upset and she didn't want to break down on national television. Especially not in front of Stacey, who she knew would take great delight in asking her more pointed questions, or in front of Pat. She wanted to get away from the cameras, away from the scrutiny. The interview had been a mistake.

And perhaps the relationship with Pat had also been a mistake. Hearing him say he wasn't looking for anything serious hurt her more than it should have, given that she had been telling herself the same thing. But hearing him say it had made her realise just how invested she had become. How much she cared for him. How much she wanted to think this could be the real thing.

She was shaking as the crew removed the microphone that was pinned to her shirt. She wasn't sure if she was angry or upset. Or both.

The drive back to Pat's house passed in an uncomfortable silence. Charli wanted to know what Pat was thinking but she was too much of a coward to ask.

He'd had ample opportunity over the past few weeks to tell her that she was special to him and he hadn't done it, and he'd made it perfectly clear tonight that she wasn't anywhere near the top of his list.

Would she have contemplated staying if he'd asked her to?

She shook her head in silent admonition. It was a ridiculous notion to entertain, it was obvious he would never ask. He had other priorities and Charli didn't need or want to compete with Ella and she couldn't compete with Margie.

How did you compete with a ghost?

She had only one option and that was to leave.

She went straight to her room and closed the door when they got home. She didn't want Pat to see her tears.

The pain in her chest was so intense she thought her heart might be breaking and for the first time since she'd left the hospital she slept alone.

* * *

'Thank you for meeting me.' Charli greeted Harriet with a hug. 'I wanted to say goodbye in person.'

'Goodbye?' Harriet let her go and stepped back. 'You're leaving?'

Charli nodded. 'I got the all clear to fly yesterday. I've booked my flight home.'

'But what about Patrick?' Harriet was frowning as she sat down. 'I thought things were going well... I thought the two of you... I don't know, did I get it wrong?'

'No, you didn't, but I think I might have.'

'What's happened?'

Nothing had happened. Or rather nothing had changed. That was the problem.

'Nothing' she said. 'Things just aren't quite what I imagined.'

Things had been awkward since the interview. Charli had waited, hoping that Pat might say something, anything, about his feelings for her, but he'd remained silent. She could only assume that his feelings were nothing more than superficial. That she was nothing more than a temporary person in his life.

'Are you sure?'

'I'm sure.' She nodded. 'I have to go.'

'You don't love him?'

She shook her head. It wasn't a question of her feelings for him. It was a question of his feelings for her. 'No.' She felt like crying but she had to stay strong. 'It doesn't matter how I feel.' She sighed. 'I don't think he can love me.'

'What does that mean?'

'I don't think he'll let himself love me. Or anyone. I think he's still in love with Ella's mother.'

'Has he told you that?'

'Not in so many words but I can hear it in the way he speaks about her and there are photos of her all over the house. She's everywhere you look. And Ella is a constant reminder of her too.'

'Charli, I saw the interview. I've seen the two of you together. Are you sure you're not in love?'

'I can't compete with a dead wife.' She wanted to be enough for someone. She didn't want to be second best.

She'd made up her mind. She had to go. This was the right decision. For all of them.

She couldn't risk her heart. Both Pat and Ella had got under her defences. Tears welled in her eyes as she thought of the little girl with her dark curls and mischievous smile, the way her warm little hand would slide into Charli's when she wasn't looking and not let go. She hadn't wanted to get attached, she'd been terrified she'd screw everything up if she did, but it had happened regardless.

'I can't stay. I have to leave before I get in any deeper. Before it hurts too much.'

Her heart was already breaking but there was no other choice.

Pat felt it as soon as he walked in the door. The air was still and quiet and the house was silent. Much too silent.

He called out to Charli but was greeted only by more silence and he knew the house was empty.

He went to her room. The door was ajar, her bed stripped bare, her sheets folded on the end of the mattress. On top of the sheets was an envelope with his name on it.

His hand shook as he opened the flap.

He didn't need to read the words. He knew what she would say.

She was gone.

He knew her flight left today but he hadn't

thought she would leave without saying good-bye. He hadn't thought she would take a taxi to the airport to avoid saying farewell, but her letter told him that was exactly what she had done.

He sat on the bed and reread her note but it gave no more clue as to what she was thinking. No more clue as to why she had left this way.

It didn't matter. It didn't change the fact that she was gone.

She had left him. And it was his fault.

But there was nothing else he could have done. Nothing he could have changed. He wasn't ready. Despite the fact that he was happy with her, he wasn't in a place where he could give his heart away again.

He'd been worried about getting too close. Worried about letting Charli into their lives, into his heart. He knew Ella had already opened her heart to her. His daughter was going to be distraught and that was his fault too. But there was nothing he could do.

He knew she couldn't stay and it wasn't fair to ask her to. He couldn't make a commitment or a promise. He couldn't offer her anything.

But he couldn't let her go without one last goodbye.

Saying goodbye was going to hurt but he would get over it. He'd got through worse.

He spotted her just as she was about to go through Security.

'Charli.' He resisted the urge to reach out and grab her, to physically stop her from taking another step.

She turned at the sound of his voice. 'Pat! What are you doing here?'

Her eyelids were puffy and the tip of her nose was red. Had she been crying? He wanted to pull her into his arms, to ask her what was wrong, but her posture was stiff and she had her arms crossed protectively over her chest. Was she protecting herself from him? He wasn't sure he could blame her.

He wanted to embrace her but instead he put his hand under her elbow and gently drew her out of the queue as he stepped backwards. 'Were you really planning on leaving without a word?' he asked.

'I thought we'd said all we had to say.'

'What about "Goodbye"?'

'You knew I was going. I'm no good at goodbyes.'

'What am I supposed to tell Ella?'

She shook her head. 'I don't know. Tell her I'm sorry.' She looked over his shoulder and he knew she was looking at the departures board. Was she really leaving? 'Pat, I have to go.'

I don't want you to. The words were on the tip of his tongue but he bit them back. Those words would get them nowhere. He couldn't ask her to stay.

She had a job to go back to. A life. A life that didn't include him.

He wanted to ask her to stay but the words lodged in his throat, choking him. He had nothing to offer her.

'Pat?' She watching him, her blue eyes big and bright. 'What are you really doing here? Is there something more you wanted to say?'

He wasn't ready but he was desperate. He took a deep breath. 'What if you stayed?'

'Stayed? Why would I stay? My future is in England. My career is there. My life is there.'

'Stay for Ella. Stay for me.'

'You said yourself there's no one important in your life other than Ella. We had fun, but we were always on a time limit. We were never supposed to have more than this.'

'If you leave now, we'll never know.'

She was shaking her head and he knew he was losing her. 'I can't be the person you want me to be.'

'What the hell does that mean?'

'I can't be Margie.'

'I don't want you to be Margie!'

'Maybe not, but I don't think you're ready for me or anyone else to take her place. You're still in love with her. You haven't moved on. You're not ready to move on. To let go.'

'That's ridiculous.'

'Is it? The house is like a shrine to her. Have you changed anything since she died?'

'No, but that wasn't for my sake or because I couldn't bear to. It was because I wanted to keep things consistent for Ella.' He hadn't been able to put away Margie's photos but he didn't even notice them any more.

'I'm sorry, Pat. I really like you and I did wish that what we had could develop into something more but I'm not ready and neither are you. There's no room for me. You told me you thought it would be you and Ella now, a unit of two, and I'm not going to come into your lives uninvited. I don't want to screw things up for Ella, like my stepmother did for me. I don't want Ella to hate me.'

'Ella loves you.'

He could make it all about Ella but they both knew that wasn't it.

'I'm not going to live in Margie's shadow. I'm not going to compete with her. You're not ready to include me in your life, not in the way I want.'

'What is it that you want?'

'I want what you and Margie had. I want to be somebody's special person.'

'Just give me some time,' he pleaded.

She shook her head. 'I haven't got time. I have to think about what is right for me. Ella will always come first in your life. Which is the way it should be, but I can't accept being anything less than second. And if I'm not going to be second then I'm not the right person for you. I'm not enough.'

He had to let her go. He had no choice. He couldn't tell her what she wanted to hear. The three words that he knew she deserved.

He'd been scared to love her in case it didn't work out, but he was going to lose her anyway.

The queue through Security was short. She stepped back into line and he watched her walk away. She didn't look back.

He'd asked her to stay and she'd shut him down.

It was over.

CHAPTER TEN

'HEY, HOW'RE THINGS at home?'

Charli kicked her shoes off and lay back on her bed as she answered her sister's phone call.

'It doesn't feel like home,' she admitted. She had been living with her father, Victoria and their newborn twins, her half-brothers, since she'd returned to England. It wasn't ideal but she'd been living with Hugo, now her ex-boyfriend, before she'd fled to Australia and she'd had nowhere else to go when she'd got back.

'No, I guess it wouldn't,' Amy said.

She and Amy hadn't lived at their father's house for years so she could understand why Amy would agree with her, but it wasn't the unfamiliar house that was the problem. The whole country felt foreign to her now. England didn't feel like home any more. She'd felt like she'd left home behind when she'd left Australia, even though she knew it wasn't the country she was missing. It was the people.

'You haven't had any luck finding something else?' Amy asked.

'No. I haven't had time to look. I'm working eighty-plus hours a week and studying.' She also hadn't been in the right frame of mind to look for alternatives. She knew she'd have to bite the bullet eventually, she couldn't stay at her father's indefinitely, but she didn't have the energy to do anything about it.

She was miserable, exhausted and lonely. She didn't *want* to start over with new flatmates, she wanted to be with Pat and Ella, but she'd mucked that up.

She missed Amy but she was missing Pat even more. Now that she was on the other side of the world she couldn't really remember why she'd left.

Nothing made sense without him.

Now that she was on her own she was acutely aware of the hole in her life. She supposed she would find something or someone else to fill it eventually, but she had come to the realisation that she didn't want to. She wanted Pat. She should have fought harder, been tougher, been braver. She should have given him more time. But none of those realisations were any use to her now.

'How are the twins?' Amy wanted to know.

'Good.' She couldn't pretend she didn't adore the babies. Despite her protests, she had fallen in love with Milo and Louis the minute she'd first held them.

'Victoria is coping okay with the whole baby thing?'

'I have to admit she's actually doing well but the nanny is a huge help. Maybe Dad should have employed nannies for us instead of marrying Victoria.'

'He did. We had a succession of them. Don't you remember?'

'No, I don't.'

'None of them stayed long. I think we were difficult and so was Dad. I don't think we can blame Victoria. She had a lot to deal with, a lot to sort out. But, tell me, how's work going?'

'It's okay.'

'Only okay?'

'It's pretty exhausting, to be honest. I'm really tired and finding it hard to focus. I feel a bit out of control.'

'I'm sure it's not that bad.'

'Adjusting to life back here *and* to work is a lot harder than I thought it would be.'

'Oh, Charli, give yourself a break. You've been through a lot of stress over the past few months—breaking up with Hugo, the landslide, leaving Pat, starting a new job—that's more than enough to deal with. Give yourself time to settle into the job, don't be so hard on yourself. Have you caught up with any of your friends?'

'I don't really feel up to it.'

'You should make an effort. I'm sure you'd feel brighter if there was something to look forward to other than work and going home. I wish I was there with you. I'd *make* you go out.'

'When will you be back?'

'I don't know. Dan has asked me to go to Canada with him. We talked about doing the winter there and he wants me to go home with him first to meet his family.'

'Really? That's great.'

She tried to be happy for Amy. Her sister had always been more adventurous, unlike Charli she'd never been afraid to take chances, but hearing Amy's plans just reinforced to her how alone she was. All she really wanted was someone to love her. Someone who wanted to share a future with her. She wanted to matter. She wanted to be the most important person to someone. But it hadn't worked out that way for her with Hugo or with Pat.

'Maybe I could come via England?' Amy was saying.

'No, don't be silly.' Charli didn't want Amy to change her plans for her. She was a grown-up, she could manage. She'd have to manage. 'I'm fine. I'm just a bit sad.'

'What's the matter?'

'I miss Pat,' she admitted. 'Now that I'm here I wish I hadn't left.'

'Oh, Charli. You should have stayed. You *could* have stayed. Why didn't you?'

'I was scared.'

'Of what?'

'Of falling in love with him. He didn't feel the same way about me. He told me, more than once, that he and Ella were a unit of two, that he wasn't looking for anything serious, but I didn't listen.' She hadn't listened to Pat or to Amy or to herself. Instead she'd given her heart away again and hoped he'd change his mind. But he hadn't. 'I thought it was better to leave. I thought I'd get over him. But it's not getting better.'

'Why don't we make plans to meet up in Canada?'

'I've only just started work, I couldn't ask for time off.'

'What about stress leave? Surely with everything you've been through, that would be a reasonable request? You could come back to Australia. There's going to be a memorial service at Wombat Gully for the victims of the landslide. You could come for that.'

'No. I don't think so.' She couldn't go back.

'Are you sure? It would give you a chance to see Pat.'

'Will he be there?'

'I'm not sure but I'd imagine he'd try.'

No, she wouldn't go back. She'd made her position totally clear to Pat. Maybe fate had brought them together but it hadn't been for the reasons she wanted. Their timing had sucked but the ball had been in Pat's court. He hadn't been ready to move on and there was no reason to think he'd changed his mind.

Pat and Connor strapped themselves into their harnesses and double- and triple-checked the carabiners, lines and anchor points before abseiling down the side of the mountain. It was the first time they'd been back to Wombat Gully since the landslide and the memories were threatening to overwhelm him.

Work had been his saving grace over the past two months. Keeping busy kept his mind occupied, but he hadn't counted on being back in Wombat Gully, back where it had all begun.

He focussed hard to block out thoughts of Charli. The two teenaged snowboarders who'd got disoriented during a blizzard and had fallen into a crevice deserved his full attention.

His feet hit the side of the mountain and he bent his knees, absorbing the impact, before he pushed off again, swinging out and releasing the line, repeating the process until finally he was at the bottom of the gully.

They found the boys in good spirits considering their ordeal and, incredibly, with relatively minor injuries. The assessments were simple enough—one dislocated shoulder with an accompanying concussion and one fractured ankle.

The dislocated shoulder had been out of

place for too long to be safely reduced in the field but Pat and Connor stabilised the broken ankle before calling for the stretchers.

They carefully lifted the boys onto the stretchers, securing them firmly before attaching the ropes and pulleys and calling for them to be winched up. Pat accompanied one boy, Connor the other, and once they reached the top a second team of Special Ops paramedics took over to transfer the boys down the mountain before they would be airlifted to Melbourne.

Pat jumped into an over-snow vehicle that would drop him and Connor off at the resort medical centre. He looked out the window as they drove past the site of the landslide. It was almost unrecognisable as the same place. The debris had been cleared and the slope was covered with snow. It was pristine and white. All traces of the disaster had been wiped clean but Pat could close his eyes and recall what it had been like. Just like he could close his eyes and remember Charli.

He opened his eyes as the over-snow transport vehicle came to a stop. As he climbed out he almost collided with Amy.

'Pat!'

The siblings were so similar that for a moment he'd thought she was Charli. He bit back his disappointment as she hugged him. He was surprised. He hadn't been sure of his reception given the way things had ended between him and her sister. 'Were you part of the rescue team?'

He nodded.

'I hear it went well.'

He nodded again. News travelled quickly around the resort.

'And how are you?' Amy asked him.

'Good,' he replied, even though it was a complete lie. He was barely coping. Charli had been gone for almost two months and he still wasn't used to her absence. He couldn't work out how a woman who had been in his life for a few weeks was managing to leave such a hole in his world.

He hadn't come to terms with the fact that he'd let her go. That he'd thought it was the best thing for both of them. That he'd thought he'd get over her quickly—after all, they hadn't had long together—but he hadn't been able to get her of his mind and he wondered how long it would take before he would stop thinking about her at all.

'How is Charli?'

The words were spoken before he'd had time to think and now they were out he wasn't sure if he wanted to hear the answer. What if Amy told him that Charli had met someone else? He wanted her to be happy but he didn't want her to have forgotten him. He didn't want her to have moved on already. She might have accused him of not moving on fast enough after Margie's death, and he knew that he couldn't compare what he and Charli had had to his wife's death, but, in many ways, he felt the loss just as keenly and part of him, selfishly, he knew, hoped that Charli was missing him just as much.

'She's sad. She misses you.'

'Did she tell you that?'

'Yes.'

'Why didn't she tell me?'

'I don't know. I think she was afraid.'

'Of what?'

'Afraid you wouldn't want her. She doesn't handle rejection well, she's been like that since our mother died, and it makes it hard for her to open up, to give her heart.'

Amy's words made sense. He had rejected her. He'd been afraid to let her in. Now all he wanted to do was to be able to take her in his arms. He wanted to protect her, to look after her. She'd gotten into his mind, his body and his heart, and his heart ached with longing.

No, it was more than that. His heart ached with love.

He closed his eyes as the realisation sank in. He loved her.

He opened his eyes as the pain sat heavily in his chest. 'I should never have let her go.'

'Maybe you should tell her that.'

He nodded. Amy was right.

He knew what he had to do. He just hoped he hadn't left it too late.

Charli signed out of her emails, closing Amy's latest message before she was tempted to make a rash decision. Amy had sent her the details of the memorial service to be held in Wombat Gully, asking her again if she thought she might return for it, but there was no way she could go. She couldn't go back.

She closed her laptop and went to check on the twins. The nanny had the night off and Charli had offered to babysit as her father and

Victoria had a function to attend. It was a rare night off for Charli too but she'd had no other plans. She was too tired to go out and she wasn't really in the right frame of mind anyway. She wasn't feeling at all sociable. Wondering vaguely if she was depressed, perhaps suffering from post-traumatic stress disorder, she knew that really all she needed was time to get over Pat. What she didn't know was how *much* time she needed.

Babysitting wasn't affecting her plans at all. She climbed the stairs to the twins' bedroom. She'd check the boys and then put the kettle on, but her plans were abandoned when she opened the door and saw Milo's bassinette shaking violently.

'Oh, my God.' She sprinted across the room and peered into the cot.

Milo was convulsing. His little face was red and she could hear him gasping for air.

She had swaddled him in a light muslin wrap to settle him but it had come loose. She unwrapped him and stripped off his leggings.

He stopped twitching as she undressed him but then his limbs went stiff and his eyes rolled back in his head. His chest was still.

He'd stopped breathing.

Charli picked him up and he lay limply in her arms as she felt for a pulse. It was there, just.

She carried him to an armchair and laid him on her lap before she bent her head and puffed a couple of breaths into his mouth.

She pulled her phone from her pocket and dialled 999. Tears ran down her cheeks as she waited for the operator to connect her to the ambulance service. She tapped the speaker option and breathed for Milo again.

She heard the call connect.

'I have an infant who is having a seizure. Prem baby, four months old, adjusted age, eleven weeks. He is febrile, unresponsive and not breathing.' She listened to the ambulance operator's questions and then continued, 'I'm performing CPR. Please send help.'

She knew the ambulance would come quickly, infants were a top priority, but she stayed on the phone until she heard the siren. It was still faint in the distance when she managed to get Milo breathing again. She hung up the phone as she quickly checked on the still-sleeping Louis, then, on shaky legs, she carried Milo carefully downstairs to open the front door.

She handed him over to the paramedics as she gave them his neonatal history and then she stood and listened and watched as they assessed Milo.

'Heart sounds normal. Left lung a little crackly. Oxygen sats ninety-eight. Pulse one hundred and forty-four. Resps thirty. Blood sugar sixty-six.' The paramedics rattled off Milo's stats.

She tasted salt on her lips and wiped her face, surprised to find the tears were still rolling down her cheeks. 'Is he going to be okay?'

'I think so.' One of the paramedics glanced up at her, a flicker of concern on his face, and Charli panicked. 'Why don't you take a seat for a moment?' he suggested, and she realised his concern was for her. She must look a complete fright.

'We'll need to take him to hospital for assessment,' the second paramedic said. 'You can come with us.'

Charli took a moment to process the information. As a doctor, she knew that would be the protocol but it seemed that when the patient was family her brain was having even more trouble than normal focussing. 'There's another baby.'

'Another one?'

'Another boy. They're twins.' She realised she wasn't being very clear.

'Is he okay?'

'He was sleeping when I checked him so I think so.'

'Where is he?'

'Upstairs. I'll need to get him. There's no one else here.'

She ran back up to the nursery and picked up Louis. She was numb as she climbed into the ambulance holding Louis, but she managed to call her father and had got herself together by the time the ambulance pulled into the hospital emergency bay.

According to the attending paramedic, Milo hadn't had any further seizures and to look at him now he seemed perfectly healthy. The medical staff took over, taking both babies as a precaution. Charli paced the waiting-room floor, hoping it was nothing sinister, as she waited for her father.

'Where is he? Is he all right?' Victoria burst into the emergency department, her eyes wild.

'He's with one of the doctors,' Charli managed to say before of the nurses intervened.

Charli listened as the nurse calmly explained to Jack and Victoria what was happening. 'Your little boy is just being assessed. The doctors will try to determine the cause of the seizure and of his temperature. Hopefully it was just a febrile seizure, caused by his high temperature. That type of seizure is common in infants.'

'What about Louis? Is he going to have a fit as well?' Victoria turned to Charli. 'Where is he?' she asked, only just realising that he was missing.

'He's here. They're both with the doctors. Louis is fine, they're just being cautious,' she said.

'I'll take you through to them now,' the nurse said to Jack and Victoria.

Charli knew there would be a raft of tests. Now that her initial panic had subsided she could recall the protocols. While the chances of Milo's seizure being related to his temperature were high, the doctors would want to rule out other causes. They would order EEGs, EKGs, blood tests and possibly an echocardiogram. She knew they would also test for meningococcal disease.

The doctors and nurses would explain all of that to Jack and Victoria. There was nothing more she could do here except wait. Her father and Victoria had each other. They didn't need her.

But she couldn't go. Not just yet. She needed to know what was happening. She sat down to wait and eventually her father reappeared.

He seemed to have aged ten years in just a few moments. He collapsed into the chair beside her.

Charli put her hand on his. She wished they had the sort of relationship where she could hug him spontaneously, he looked like he could use a hug, but since her mother had died they had never been demonstrative. 'How is he?'

'The doctors have put him on precautionary antibiotics and they're waiting for test results but they seem hopeful that it's not meningococcal. Hopefully it's nothing more than a fever. I really hope so. I don't think I could handle anything more. Not on top of losing your mother and then almost losing you.'

Charli was momentarily taken aback. It

was the first time her father had given any indication that past events had upset him.

'These boys are my second chance,' he continued.

'At what?'

'At being a decent father.'

'I didn't realise you had any regrets.'

'I have plenty of regrets, Charlotte, my girl. I was devastated when your mother died. I completely fell apart, I had depression for a long time. I was barely coping when I met Victoria. She insists I *wasn't* coping. I was drinking heavily, it wasn't a healthy environment for the two of you. It wasn't a happy home. I needed time to heal and to recover. To learn how to cope. We thought boarding school would give you a safer, more stable environment. I thought I'd have time to make it up to you, to explain why I'd made that decision, but the years went past and I missed my chance. I thought I'd be able to be a father to you again but you'd grown up and didn't need me.'

'We always needed you, Dad.'

'I have lost a wife and lost touch with my daughters. I wish I could have my time again. I would do things differently. I love

Victoria and I love the boys but I have never stopped loving you. I was distraught when your mother died, there went all my hopes and dreams for our future, but I appreciate how lucky I am to have had the love of two women in my life. Sometimes it still feels like your mother died yesterday. It's strange to think I've been married to Victoria for longer than your mother and I were married.'

Charli had never thought about her father's two marriages in terms of years of commitment. In her mind her mother was his first wife, which mentally elevated her status in Charli's opinion, but her father was right. His second marriage had lasted much longer. She should be glad that he'd found happiness a second time. She *was* glad.

Maybe it was possible to love more than one person.

She turned to her father. 'Can I ask you a question?' When he nodded, she continued, 'Did you love them the same or do you love Victoria differently?'

'The love is different in a way because your mother and Victoria are different and because my life was different when I met Victoria. I didn't think I would fall in love again, I wasn't in the right place mentally for a long time, but when I met Victoria I knew she was my second chance and that I couldn't let her go. I was older, wiser, and I'd learnt the hard way to make the most of my opportunities. I hadn't expected to love again and I think I appreciate it more because of what I had already lost. But it's not a case of loving one more than the other. I love them both, but only one of them is here.'

'I'm glad you found love again, Dad.'

'And what about you, my girl? Are you happy?'

'No, not really.' Charli shook her head as she fought back the tears that seemed perpetually too close to the surface of late. 'I miss Patrick.'

'Why didn't you stay with him?'

'I had a job to come back to.'

'Surely you could have delayed your start date?'

'I suppose so but I couldn't stay. I didn't think he could love me the way he loved his wife.' But listening to her father talk, maybe she'd been wrong about that. Maybe she should have given him time.

'Do you love him?'

She nodded.

'Have you told him that?'

'No. I was afraid to.'

'It's not too late to tell him how you feel. You only get one shot at life but if you are lucky you get a second shot at love. If he's lucky, he'll get you.'

'You think I should tell him how I feel?'

'What have you got to lose?'

Her father was right. She'd already lost everything. She had nothing more to lose and everything to gain.

Wombat Gully was serene and still. The ski runs had closed for the day, the lifts were quiet, the season almost over. Most people would probably be glad for this season to end. The site of the landslide had been cleared and a pathway laid up the side of the hill, leading to the newly erected monument that marked the tragedy.

Charli negotiated the path, stopping at each bend to take in the views over the valley. The path had been built to encourage people to pause and look out, to look away from the mountain and out to the horizon. For Charli the view was a window to the future.

The memorial service was scheduled for tomorrow morning at eleven but Charli wanted to visit the memorial alone. At sunset. It seemed like the most appropriate time.

She needed some time to compose herself. Not for the memorial service but for the possibility that she might see Pat tomorrow. She had no idea if he planned to attend the service but if he wasn't there she would go to Melbourne next. She wasn't leaving Australia again without seeing him.

She hoped she might not have to leave again at all.

Charli reached the top of the path and stopped in front of the memorial. It was a simple structure made of stone and wood and metal. She ran her fingers over the fifteen names etched into the metal before sitting at the base of the monument. She turned her back to the path and faced west towards the setting sun.

'Charli?'

She almost didn't turn around, thinking she was imagining the sound of her name, but then she heard it again.

'Charli?'

She looked up, not quite able to believe what she was seeing.

'Pat!'

He was smiling at her and his arms were open. Before his smile had time to stretch across his face Charli was on her feet and in his arms. He scooped her up and she buried her face into the curve of his jaw, inhaling his scent. Tears flooded her eyes. It felt so good, *he* felt so good. He felt like home.

He set her down on her feet but kept his hands on her waist, keeping her close. She tipped her head back to look at him and lifted her hand to his face, checking that he was real. The dark stubble of his beard grazed her palm as he turned his head and kissed the soft flesh at the base of her thumb. Her stomach flipped as his lips grazed her skin. He was definitely real.

'What are you doing here?'

She had spent the hours of the long plane flight working out what she wanted to say but now that he was standing in front of her she couldn't remember how, or where, she'd planned to start. Her heart was pounding and her body trembled a little with nerves.

She looked up at him, at his familiar

smile, and as she looked into his green eyes the fog that had surrounded her for the past few weeks lifted. Her world was suddenly brighter and her outlook immediately seemed more positive. She still had no idea how he did it, how he had *such* an effect on her and her sense of well-being, but just having him there, with his arms around her, made her feel as though there was light at the end of the dark tunnel she had found herself in.

He looked pleased to see her but was he ready to hear what she had to say? She had to take the chance.

'I came to see you,' she said. Encouraged by his smile, she continued, 'Getting on the plane to go back to England was the hardest thing I've ever done. I thought it would be okay because it was my choice, I thought it wouldn't hurt so much because *I* was the one leaving, but I hadn't counted on leaving my heart behind. I told myself I was going off to a new job, a new future, a new life, but it wasn't the future or life I wanted.'

'No?'

She shook her head. 'No.'

'What do you want?'

'I want you. I want us. I want a chance at being together, in whatever form that takes.'

'Are you sure?'

'I'm positive. And there's more I need to say. Even if it's still too soon for you or if you don't think we have a future, I can't leave things unsaid. I need to be brave. I need to know that I've gone after what I want. You might not want another wife. You might not want a stepmother for Ella but I want a chance to be a part of your life. To be with you. I love you.'

He cupped her chin with his fingers and tilted her face up to his. He bent his head and covered her lips with his. He wrapped his right arm around her waist and pulled her to him and kissed her firmly. She closed her eyes as she tasted him, as she melted into his embrace, surrendering to his touch, as everything came rushing back. He was so familiar. He was home.

God, she'd missed him.

Her lips were swollen and cold as his mouth left hers but his fingers traced the curve of her face. 'I can't believe you are here,' he said. 'Do you know, I was planning on coming to you?'

'To me?'

He nodded. 'I was just trying to work out the logistics of time off and who would look after Ella and then I was coming to find you.'

'Why?'

'To tell you I never should have let you go. I didn't realise what I was losing when I let you go. I want more time with you, time to make a new life, new memories, a future. I lost the chance to make something special with you and I had no idea how much it would hurt, what it would cost me to say goodbye. I will always love Margie, she's part of who I am, she's part of Ella too, but she's also part of my past. *You* are my future and I love you.'

'You love me?'

'I do.' He nodded again and wrapped her in his arms, his hug familiar, warm and comforting, and there was nowhere else she wanted to be. 'I should have asked you to stay but I didn't think I could. I didn't think it was fair to ask you to give up everything and take us on. I knew you had reservations about being a stepmother and I think you had reservations about me too.'

'I would have stayed if you'd said you loved

me but I didn't think you really needed me. I didn't think I would ever be important enough and I didn't want to be second best. But I've regretted leaving ever since. It was a mistake. I missed you and I should have told you how I felt.'

'You're not second best.'

'It's okay. I'm happy to be second to Ella. She *should* be the most important person in your life, she deserves that, it's what I always wanted from my own father. I just need to be in your heart too.'

'You are definitely in my heart. I loved Margie and I love Ella but I also love you. Love isn't finite,' he said. 'I'm not afraid to love again. There's room in my heart for all of you. Do you trust me?'

'With my life. You saved me once already.'

'Then trust that I need you in my life. I fell for you the moment I first saw you and I started to fall in love with you and your courage and your spirit while you were trapped, and then I continued to fall in love with you a little more each day, but I didn't realise it until you left me. Until I was trying to live without you. I don't *want* to live my life without you. I love you and I want us to be together.

I want you to share your life with me. And Ella. With us.'

'Do you think I can do it? Do you think I can be a stepmother? I haven't had a great experience.'

'I know you're worried about that but Ella adores you and she doesn't need a stepmother. She needs a mother. All you need to do is love her. She doesn't remember Margie and that's something that I had to learn to deal with, but I don't want her to forget you too. I don't want to lose you as well. I want to spend my life with you. I want a future with you. We'll figure it all out. Together.'

As the sun dipped below the mountains and the sky turned pink Pat dropped to one knee and held her hands. 'Charli, I want to give you the peace, stability, happiness and love that you deserve. Will you do me the honour of becoming my wife? Will you love me and Ella? Will you make us a family? Will you marry me?'

Charli beamed as she pulled him to his feet. She had tears of happiness in her eyes as she said simply, 'I will.'

She tilted her face up and kissed him, savouring the feel of his lips on hers. She'd had a million questions but none of them seemed important any more.

Patrick loved her. Nothing else mattered.

EPILOGUE

'ARE YOU READY?'

Charli heard her father's voice as he knocked on the closed door.

'I'm ready.'

Charli couldn't keep the smile off her face. She was getting married. Patrick was waiting for her at the edge of the lake. She felt as if she were dreaming. She could hardly believe that she could be so lucky. That this was actually happening. There had been no disasters. Everything had gone seamlessly.

She ran her hands down the front of her wedding dress, smoothing out the non-existent creases.

Harriet and Amy kissed her on her cheek and wished her well before leaving her to have a few minutes alone with her father. They had helped her to get ready, doing her hair and make-up and buttoning her into her dress. Butterflies danced in her belly as she thought about the person who would help her to undress later. She knew how lucky she was to be surrounded by friends and family, people who loved her, and she was so grateful. She was thankful that she'd been rescued and that Pat had been patient and taught her how to love him.

'Charlotte, you look beautiful. So like your mother.'

She knew she looked like her mother but today she was going to let that support her and give her strength. She was happy and ready for the next stage in her life. She had completed one year as a medical officer at the Princess Elizabeth Hospital, working with Harriet and the medical staff who had looked after her following the landslide. She was loving her career and had been accepted into GP training in Victoria but she was also ready now to become a wife and mother. With Pat beside her, she was ready for anything.

'He's a good man, your Patrick, and a lucky one to have found you. I know you'll both be very happy.'

Charli could see tears in his eyes. She wasn't going to lose it before she got married. Today was a day for smiles, laughter and happiness.

'Thanks, Dad.' She tucked her arm into the crook of his elbow and kissed his cheek. 'Shall we go?'

Pat's mum was waiting outside the door with a very excited Ella.

Charli stepped out onto the wide veranda of the lake house and looked down to the water. White wooden chairs had been set out in rows facing the lake and the guests had taken their seats. She was vaguely aware of Pat's father and Victoria in the first row with the twins who, amazingly for fifteen-month-old boys, were actually sitting still. Daniel sat alongside Victoria and Charli knew he'd have his eyes on Amy. She looked for Harriet among the hospital staff but saw her sitting with Pat's paramedic mates. Interesting, she thought with a smile.

The string quartet from the local high school began to play and the guests all swivelled in their seats, turning to look at the bride, but now Charli only had eyes for Pat.

He was standing at the end of the grassy aisle on the bank of the lake under the wooden arch that she had watched him build. Heat flushed her cheeks as she thought about those late autumn weekends when he'd worked bare-chested in the sun, building the arbour.

He was flanked by his brother and Amy and he was smiling at her as he waited, and Charli had to stop herself from running to him and throwing herself into his arms. Looking at him now, she couldn't believe she had once been scared to love him. She was a different person from the one he had first met. She was confident, secure, loved and happy. He had taught her how to open her heart and how to love.

Ella was getting impatient. 'Now, Charli?' she asked as she tugged on her hand.

Charli nodded and Ella took off down the wooden steps and skipped along the aisle, scattering pink and white rose petals from her basket. Charli and her father followed at a slightly more sedate pace.

Pat scooped Ella up when she got to the arbour and gave her a kiss before setting her down at his side. Charli passed Ella her bouquet to hold and Pat shook Jack's hand before taking Charli's hands in his.

He was grinning at her, his green eyes

sparkling with love. 'Do you want to get married now?' he asked.

Charli smiled back at him. 'I do.'

Pat leant in and kissed her as the celebrant cleared her throat. 'I think you're getting a little ahead of yourselves,' she said with a smile, but Charli didn't care. She was ready to marry Pat, ready to start their life together, ready to be a family.

'I love you,' she whispered to him. 'I will always love you.'

* * * * *